FESTIVAL FIREWORKS

ANN BURNETT

LADYBUG PUBLICATIONS

ISBN: 9780955854088

Ebook first published 2018

Published by Ladybug Publications.

To the men in my life. They know who they are.

1

The sounds and smells she woke to were different. No raucous shrieks of pink and grey galahs decorating the gums like blossom, or her mother's voice calling to the chooks to be fed in the yard. No smell of coffee brewing in the kitchen or the hint of jasmine and bougainvillea through the open window.

Instead, the whine of car engines as they crawled up the Canongate, squeezing past each other just outside her window, the chatter of early risers on their way to work, the clatter of shop shutters being raised. The smells, the strange smells of old, musty history still present in the ancient buildings, of long ago lives, dark deeds and secret trysts, mingled with traffic fumes and last night's cooking.

Jill opened her eyes and a smile swept over her face. Edinburgh at last. Half the world away from where she had been forty-eight hours ago. In the bright summer light of morning, she looked around at her Aunt Linda's bedroom from beneath the warmth of her duvet. Last night when she arrived, she had been too exhausted to do anything but to fall into a soft, creaky, but very welcome bed. Now she took the time to scrutinise the room. There was a large, dark wood wardrobe, the handles tied together with blue ribbon, a matching dressing table with three drawers all of which had corners of material bulging out, a bedside table with a lamp whose dusty shade hung awry and several unmatched wooden chairs. And everywhere, books. Piles of books tottered on the chairs, books obscured all but a few inches of the mirror on the dressing table, books piled higgledy-piggledy on the floor, even the top of the wardrobe was packed to the ceiling with them.

At least I won't be short of reading material, Jill thought.

Some of the book piles were decorated with overspill from the wardrobe: a black hat with a huge brim and diamanté and feather trim; several frothy scarves in a spectrum of colours; a large brown handbag packed with pairs of gloves, their fingers poking up like sea anemones; an enamelled box overflowing with paste jewellery.

And Jill had thought her aunt had brought enough luggage for six when she arrived to stay with her sister Patricia, Jill's mum. They'd done a swap, Linda and Jill, − Linda to Jill's home in the dark green hills above the Queensland coast, and Jill to Linda's tenement flat in Edinburgh's Royal Mile. Linda was very much the younger sister to Jill's mum, being a mere 11 years old when her older sister and her new husband had emigrated to Australia. Jill had only a few days with her before she too, set off on her travels.

With a last snuggle under the cosy duvet, Jill forced herself to get up.

'Best cure for jet lag is to adjust to the local time as quickly as possible,' Linda had told her.

She showered and washed her long, fair hair free of the dust and stickiness of travel, pulled on a white t-shirt and

jeans, and wrapped a towel around her head. Slipping her
feet into a pair of battered flip-flops, she wandered into the
lounge and opened the curtains. It wasn't the most
enchanting of outlooks.

'My bedroom is at the front and the lounge is at the
back,' Linda had said, when explaining the ins and outs of
her Edinburgh home. 'I need peace to work in the daytime,
but I can sleep through anything.'

The back of the tenement building looked onto what
had been the drying green in former times, but although
the poles to hold the washing lines were still there, the area
had been tarmacked over and was now used for parking.
Linda's 'new' old car, which she'd left in the long-stay car
park at the airport, was sitting where Jill had parked it the
night before.

'I bought a new one because Percy was on his last legs,'
Linda had said. 'This one's only done 75,000 miles and
isn't too hard to get going, though it has its off days.'

Fortunately, it had started first time when Jill had finally
reached it after her epic journey across the world.

And now, it sat there, promising Jill freedom to travel
across Scotland, to see the castles and battlegrounds and
palaces she was so keen on. Edinburgh itself, as Linda had
told her, was filled with history, and she would be able to
spend many pleasant hours exploring the sights of the city.
She pulled up the old wooden sash window and leant out
on the window sill to smell the air of this new environment.
The chill of the morning air surprised her as goose bumps
rose on her bare arms. This was supposed to be summer,
wasn't it? Jill rubbed her arms to get her circulation going
and as she did so, she became aware that each parking bay
had a number and the one which matched the number of
Linda's apartment was empty.

'Oops!' she laughed. 'I'd better move Percy into his

correct space, otherwise someone is going to be mighty cross.'

Just then, a sleek, black car drove into the parking area. It came to a sudden halt behind Linda's car, and Jill saw a young man, dressed in a smart black suit, climb out and stare – angrily, judging by his stance – at her car.

He turned and, frowning up at the building, caught sight of Jill at the window.

'Is that your car?' he shouted up at her.

'Yes,' she called back.

'You can't park there!' he yelled. 'That's my space.'

'Ok, I'm sorry,' Jill called down to him. 'I didn't know. I'm new here.'

'Aren't you going to move it then?' His face glared up at her, and even from two storeys up, she could make out the flash in his dark eyes. His stance reinforced his mood, hands on hips, long legs set apart, gripping the pot-holed tarmac of the parking area with a ferocity she couldn't miss.

'I've just washed my hair. Can you give me ten minutes while I dry it?'

'No!' The bellow reverberated around the buildings. Jill could well imagine numerous faces half hidden behind twitching curtains watching and listening to the contretemps. She sighed, closed the window, and gave her wet hair another rub with the towel, then slipped on a jacket and headed for the door.

The natives don't seem all that friendly, she said to herself as she flip-flopped her way down two flights of tenement stairs. The stairs wound round and round in an open spiral, and Jill held onto the brass balustrade as she descended. Wrought iron banisters coiled in fanciful flowers below the balustrade. Someone, many years ago, had taken a lot of time and care in fashioning them, she thought.

All the way down she tried to think of smart put-downs for Mr. Bossy outside, but her brain still wasn't up to speed after her flight. At the landing window, she glimpsed him pacing up and down beside Linda's car. His Mercedes still had its engine running.

Waster, she thought, more money than sense. Using up his fuel and polluting the atmosphere. No green credentials, him.

When she opened the door into the back court, he turned towards her. She could see how tall he was now; upstairs, the height had foreshortened him.

'Thank goodness!' he exclaimed. 'Now shift your car and let me in.'

'What's the magic word?' It was out before she could think. Jill's infamous 'open mouth before engage brain' syndrome.

'Pardon?'

'No, not that but at least it's a start.'

He glowered at Jill while she tried to stand as tall and straight and important as her five feet four inches, wet hair, and flip-flops would allow. She met his eye and held her gaze.

'Don't be so childish,' he said, 'and hurry up and move your car.'

Glaring at him, Jill climbed into the driver's seat of Linda's Yaris and attempted to start it.

It coughed and died. She tried again, and the same thing happened. What had Linda said about the car? 'It was a great bargain, though it is a wee bit tetchy about starting. A touch temperamental, in fact.' Sounds like Mr. Bossy here, she thought. 'But just jolly it along a bit and it will get going.' Well, that was something she wasn't going to try with Mr. Bossy. Though the sooner he got going the better, but she decided to try it on the car.

'Come on now,' she said out loud. 'Try your best. You know you can do it.' The engine coughed and spluttered. 'That's it. That's the job. Come on, just a bit more.'

The engine caught, and she revved it up to make sure. 'Wonderful! See, I told you you could do it.'

She glanced round to see Mr. Bossy staring bemusedly at her. She wound down the window, gave him a nod, and shouted, 'No worries!' before reversing out of the space and parking in her designated bay.

She watched as he swung the sleek, black Mercedes into the spot she'd occupied. He jumped out, clicked the lock, and hurried into the entrance of the apartments.

Some colourful Aussie phrases spluttered from her at the same time as she heard Linda's voice again. 'And watch what you say,' she'd told her. 'Some of your more interesting idioms are regarded as swearing in the UK.'

Jill had a quick peek round, but she was quite alone, so she said a few more on the subject of Mr. Bossy before she climbed out of the car and flip-flopped her way back up the two flights of stairs to Linda's flat.

The brass balustrade gleamed from over a hundred years of rubbing by the hands of people climbing the stairs, or by residents polishing it.

'I won't expect you to do it,' Linda had said, 'though old Mrs. Anderson across the landing polished it every day until she died.'

Jill glanced across at what had been Mrs. Anderson's flat as she reached her own front door. Just then, the door opposite opened and out stepped Mr. Bossy, this time carrying a black briefcase and a local supermarket's bag for life, stuffed full of papers and files. Somehow it didn't quite match his well-tailored suit and highly polished black shoes.

She tried not to smile; in fact, she tried to blank him as she put the key in her lock – the wrong way. By the time she realised what she was doing, he was across the landing and standing behind her.

Was it her imagination, or was there such a heat coming from him like a furnace? She felt herself glowing from it, and she was sure her face was a bright, hot red. She turned the key this way and that, ratcheting at it in an attempt to open her door and escape his alarming presence.

'Take your time.' He spoke with that charming, musical accent, a cross between James McAvoy and Ewan MacGregor, with just a hint of Billy Connolly. 'These locks are pretty old and don't take kindly to being forced. You have to jolly them along a bit.' He paused. 'I'm Andrew, by the way. Sorry I was a bit sharp there. In a bit of a rush. I'm short-staffed. No PA to help me out.'

Jill turned to stare at him. He looked transfixed, away in a different world. At last she said, 'I think I'll manage to open the door myself. I've obviously done it before, otherwise I wouldn't be here.'

He came to, gave her a brief nod, then clattered down the stairs.

She watched him circling downwards, diminishing as he went, until all she could see was the top of his head. Not even a bald spot to smirk at, she thought, as his footsteps made towards the heavy street door and she heard it open. Briefly, the noise of the street outside bounced in and then the door closed with a thud. He was gone.

Turning to her door again, she managed to open it first time. 'Typical,' she said to herself. 'That's what he does to

me. Makes me all thumbs and fingers, and jittery, too. I'm
going to stay clear of Mr. Bossy.'

FOR HIS PART, Mr. Bossy felt anything but. He was
disturbed by this young woman, by her freshness and
strength of character. He wasn't used to girls facing up to
him, telling him off and commenting on his manners. He
strode along the Canongate, weaving in and out the many
tourists ambling along and taking in the sights.

She was nothing like Nicola in looks or demeanour, if
the contretemps in the car park was anything to go by, but
he found himself strangely drawn to her. In the soft, grey
light of the landing, she had seemed to him to be a beam
of sunshine, golden and warm, and exuding a joie de vivre.
He had taken in her sparkling green eyes flecked with gold;
long, wet hair that would be corn-coloured when it dried;
and warm, light brown skin tanned to perfection, and not
from a bottle either. He couldn't help but feel she was an
alien sprite arrived in the douce, grey world of Edinburgh.

But he couldn't, wouldn't let her into his life. He had
had enough of dealing with the emotions a woman stirred
up in him. He didn't want to get heavily involved again,
not even with this attractive one.

She was Australian, by the sound of it. No Kylie
Minogue or Nicole Kidman, though. Pretty enough, but
definitely rather too outspoken for him. And what was she
doing in Linda Naismith's flat? He knew Linda had gone
off on her travels again ('to give the muse a bit of inspira-
tion,' she called it) but he didn't remember her saying she
was renting out her flat. And her car, now that he thought
about it. It was Linda's 'new' old car she'd bought just
before she left that the girl had parked in his space.

Wait a moment. He stopped dead in the street and a

couple of Japanese tourists bumped into him. With many bows and 'so sorrys', they eventually passed him and left him recalling Linda muttering something about a niece from Australia taking a year off from teaching in the Outback. He also remembered telling Linda he'd keep an eye open for her. Oh glory, that meant he'd have to be nice to her.

'WELL,' said Jill, going into her flat. 'That is one guy I'm crossing off my Christmas card list. Grumpy or what?

After she dried her hair, leaving it floating around her like golden grass, she switched on Linda's computer to email her that she'd arrived safely. Almost as an afterthought, she added,

Who is that neighbour in the opposite flat? Andrew, he said he was called. The one with the fancy Mercedes. He was rather annoyed when I parked in his space.

By the time she'd finished breakfast and cleared up, to her own satisfaction if not her mum's – had she seen it – the reply had arrived. After filling Jill in on the finer points of living in an Edinburgh tenement flat, Linda wrote;

So, you've met my neighbour, Andrew. Isn't he lovely? I forgot to tell you we each have our own parking space. Andrew's pretty busy just now as he's involved with the Festival a lot. He said he'd keep an eye out for you. Send him my love.

Jill snorted. How different people could appear to others. He'd obviously charmed Linda. But she wasn't going to let Mr. Bossy spoil her day. She flung on her jacket, lifted her bag, and set off on foot to explore the city and the Festival.

A cacophony of sound assailed Jill as the open top, double-decker tour bus moved slowly past her in the street. At first it was all one hellish storm, but she tuned out the car horns and the squealing brakes and concentrated instead on the chatter of the crowds, here and there a burst of music, the shouts of the ticket touts.

The noise blasted off the walls of the grey sandstone buildings lining the narrow street. They stood there as impenetrable as ever, impervious to the riot of colour below.

And it *was* a riot. As the bus inched forward, a troupe of musicians dressed in bright yellow and gold wended their way towards a church whose doors stood open. The crowd barely parted to let them through, nor did they pay them more than scant attention. A balloon seller's wares floated above her, gaudy purples and reds mixed with pastel shades and black and gold. They looked like hallucinogenic grapes rubbing gently against each other.

The crowd moved in myriad directions, formless yet forming a whole. They were easy-going and easy going; only an occasional formally-dressed man or woman pushed their way through with an objective in mind. The rest didn't care where they went, letting the tide take them where it would, or else being drawn into the dark steep entrances – closes, they were called, according to the name plaques which Jill read beside each one, and which led down to the centre of the city.

Another tour bus crept alongside Jill. The tour guide's voice broke in above the noise, pointing out various historical items: this building was 500 years old; Robert Burns, the national poet, had visited here in seventeen-eighty something, Mary, Queen of Scots, had prayed in that church; Burke and Hare stole their bodies here.

It was too much to take in all at once, so Jill ordered a coffee at a cafe where she could sit outside and soak up the atmosphere, the ambience, the ethos, the vibes, until she felt more a part of it all.

No wonder Linda loves living here, she thought. All those books she writes; it must be the sea air. Linda had rattled off the names of several fictional characters spawned by other Edinburgh writers: Long John Silver was one, Jill remembered; Miss Jean Brodie; and of course, Harry Potter. But who were Inspector Rebus, Precious Ramotswe, Mark Renton? Jill determined to do a lot of reading while she was here, and find out about them.

2

The next morning after breakfast, Jill took her cup of coffee and her laptop to the dining table and looked up employment agencies for some temporary work. She had intended to have the year off to travel, but already the prices she'd seen in her exploration of the city looked prohibitive. She needed to earn something just to help her savings out.

There were quite a few employment agencies in the city, so with the help of her street map, she picked out those closest to Linda's apartment. After several phone calls to boring-sounding establishments, she hit some luck. Elite Employment were not only a few hundred yards away, but they would be pleased to see her that morning at 10.30.

Jill was galvanised into action. Tearing off her jeans and t-shirt, she opened the wardrobe and stared at the clothes she had brought with her. They fitted easily into the space Linda had cleared for her, as travelling light had been more important than being a fashion plate. Not that she'd had much chance of being that in the Kimberley in Western Australia where she had taught.

She eventually decided on a pair of black trousers and a plain white blouse. She put on a splash of make-up and perfume, brushed her long hair until it hung like a shimmering curtain, and decided she looked efficient, capable, and responsible. What she wasn't, was warm. Although it was early August, the Edinburgh 'summer' was distinctly cool. Jill looked out of the window onto the street and watched the passers-by bundled in sweaters and fleeces, and even light coats. All Jill had with her was a waterproof jacket, more suited to country walks than job interviews.

She had a sudden thought. What about Linda's clothes? I'm sure she wouldn't mind if I borrowed a jacket or a cardigan to wear. Her aunt was only 12 years older than her and, from what Jill had seen of her clothes, Linda dressed very well. Jill opened the wardrobe again and searched through the clothing.

She certainly goes for bright colours, was her thought, as she pulled out a scarlet shorty coat, a lime green and yellow shift dress, and an electric blue sweater. Then she saw a woolly jacket in soft pinks and purples. It had a small collar and a belt, and three large buttons. When she drew it on, it felt light and cosy, and fitted her perfectly.

'Thanks, Linda,' she said to herself, as she grabbed her bag and headed out to Elite Employment's offices.

She walked from the apartment up the cobbled street of the Royal Mile before she reached a building with a discreet plaque on the outside informing her she'd arrived at her destination. Jill took a moment to catch her breath before climbing the stairs to the second-floor offices.

Edinburgh people must be really fit, or at least have massive calf muscles, she reckoned, as she stood at the solid wooden door with Elite Employment in gold lettering. As instructed by a small notice, she rang the bell and went in.

A woman, who looked to be in her late fifties, smiled at her as Jill gave her name.

'I'm Nessie MacDonald. Just go in,' she said, indicating a door to her left. 'My sister is waiting for you.'

A plump woman with white hair and a close resemblance to her sister stood up and came round her desk to shake her hand.

'I'm Jessie MacDonald. Please sit down, dear,' she said, indicating a wooden chair on the opposite side of the desk to hers. 'And tell me all about yourself.'

'I'm from Australia,' Jill began, 'and I'm over here staying in my aunt's flat while she's in Oz visiting my mum. I was a teacher in the north of Western Australia for four years, but I've taken a break to travel. My mum and dad are Scottish, so I wanted to come over and see where they'd been brought up.' Jill ground to a halt and groaned inwardly. Verbal diarrhoea was taking over again. Slow down, she told herself. Take it easy.

Miss MacDonald was watching her and nodding encouragingly. Jill took a deep breath and was about to speak again, when the door opened and the other Miss MacDonald burst in.

'Oh Jessie,' she said. 'That was Mr. MacCallum-Blair on the phone. He's looking for a PA immediately. He's pretty desperate, as you can imagine.'

Jill's ears pricked up as the two sisters went into a huddle over their database of possibilities on the computer. PA? Personal assistant? Jill was ready when the two Miss MacDonalds turned to her.

'I could do that,' she told them. 'I've had quite a bit of experience.'

'Can you organise corporate events?' asked Nessie.

'Yes,' Jill replied emphatically. Well, she had organised

several beach barbecues when she was at University, the annual sports day at the school, and been on the local environmental committee.

'Have you experience of dealing with members of the public and, what you might call nowadays, celebrities?' asked Jessie.

'Loads,' replied Jill. 'I worked in customer services and also made arrangements for special guests and their entourage.' A week in a call centre, and meeting an up-and-coming boy band from the Sydney flight when they had come to Brisbane to play at the University's Christmas ball. She hoped the women wouldn't enquire too closely into it. The Premier of Western Australia had also flown up to see the flood damage to the school one year when the rains had been particularly heavy.

'And of course, I'm familiar with all things IT,' she continued, nodding in the direction of the computer. She'd made sure all the school kids had access to one as a link to the world beyond their community.

Nessie and Jessie looked at each other.

'Well,' said Jessie, 'he is desperate.'

'Yes,' agreed Nessie. 'He is.'

'Miss, er...' she glanced down at her notes. 'Miss Kennedy,' Jessie began, 'Mr. MacCallum-Blair is one of our most esteemed customers, and we wouldn't want to send him just anyone. He is an up-and-coming player in Edinburgh's cultural life, and he needs someone who is capable, responsible, and efficient.'

That describes me perfectly, Jill thought with a slight smile, remembering her choice of clothes.

'He also needs someone right away,' said Nessie.

'No worries,' said Jill. 'I can be there in two shakes of a wombat's tail.'

The MacDonald sisters looked slightly shocked.

'Sorry,' Jill said, remembering Linda's stricture regarding Aussie idioms. 'Just tell me the address and I'll be on my way.'

JILL ENJOYED the walk down The Mound and across Princes Street. The Misses MacDonald had advised her against taking the car, as parking apparently was 'a bit of a nightmare anywhere in the city'.

Mr. MacCallum-Blair's offices were situated in Edinburgh's New Town. Jill walked along a broad, leafy street, on one side of which were railed-off gardens accessible only through locked gates, and on the other an elegant row of terraced townhouses, each with its own porticoed entrance and, no doubt, a key to the garden opposite. Jill noticed that most of the properties were now given over to offices and galleries.

She wondered what Mr. MacCallum-Blair would be like. Late fifties, she thought, balding, with a large stomach and a pinstripe suit. Or perhaps fortyish with longish hair and lurid ties, a live-in girlfriend who works in advertising or as a model, and....

Jill was so busy conjuring up her new boss's lifestyle that she had passed the number before she realised it. She quickly doubled back and ran up the broad steps to the entrance to number 76. According to the nameplate, MacCallum-Blair Enterprises was on the first floor. She buzzed and gave her name, then waited for the click of the door's release.

She ran up the stairs and, as she turned to climb the final flight, she was surprised to see a woman sitting at a desk at the top of the stairs, watching her ascent.

'Good morning,' she said. 'I take it you're from the agency?'

'Yes, I'm Jill Kennedy.'

The woman nodded. 'Take a seat,' she said, gesturing at an armchair in the corner next to a coffee table of glossy magazines.

Like an upmarket dentist's, Jill thought, and I feel exactly as if I was going to have several teeth pulled.

The phone rang and, while the woman answered it, Jill took the opportunity to size her up. After all, she would probably be working quite closely with her. Early forties, neatly dressed in a dark blue trouser suit, with a pale lilac patterned blouse and wedding and engagement rings. Not the boss's fancy woman. Probably the PA she was replacing had that role. Or maybe Mr. MacCallum-Blair was happily married. Here's hoping, at any rate. She didn't fancy having to cope with amorous advances as well as the new workload.

'Mr. MacCallum-Blair will see you now.' The woman pointed to a dark wooden door. 'Just go in. He's taking a call at the moment, but he won't be long.'

Jill tapped on the door and went in. The room was dominated by two long picture windows, through which Jill could see the trees in the private gardens. A nice outlook for the boss then. In front of the windows was a wide, old-fashioned desk with a very modern laptop sitting on it. Mr. MacCallum-Blair had swivelled his chair round to face out of the window while he took the call. While he ummed and said 'Right' and 'Fine' to his caller, Jill took the opportunity to admire the high ceiling decorated with an elaborate cornice of grapes, vine leaves, and flowers, and a centrepiece, similarly decorated, surrounding the base of a chandelier.

It's stunning, she thought, as she admired the crystal pendants waterfalling from their fixture. The light from the windows caught them, and glints flashed around the ceiling and walls. She was enchanted.

'Good God, not you,' said a voice.

3

Jill was startled out of her reverie. There, behind the desk, sat Mr. Bossy. He was open-mouthed with what can only be described as shock. So was Jill. For an endless moment, neither of them could speak. Mr. MacCallum-Blair recovered first.

'Did Jessie send you?'

'Yes,' said Jill. 'She said you were desperate.'

'Not that d...' he began, suddenly remembering his manners, but not before Jill had bristled at his insult. She drew herself up and wished she'd brought her stilettos with her. At least then, she might have given the impression of towering over his desk.

'I am efficient, capable, and responsible,' she found herself saying, at the same time as a giggle threatened to burst from her throat. She swallowed it down and frowned. 'Miss MacDonald wouldn't have sent me if she didn't think I would suit you. However,' she continued, 'obviously I don't, so I won't waste any more of your time.'

She had her hand on the door handle before she heard him call her back.

'I'm sorry,' he said, looking down at his desk. 'Of course I want you to stay.'

She hesitated. Did she really want to work with him? Could she stand his high-handedness and rudeness? She would never feel that she could get away from him, living across the landing as he did. Then another little voice whispered in her ear. The money's good. You need it if you want to travel. It's only for a short while. She paused. Then she took her hand away from the handle and turned back to Mr. Bossy. Mr. Bossy the boss. Right. She'd put up with him and his appalling manners, but only until she'd earned enough to fund her trip around Scotland.

'Very well,' she said, 'I'll stay. But if, after a week, we find we are unable to work together, then I shall ask to be released from this position.' Again, a giggle rose. Was that her really speaking like that? She tried to look severe as he told her her duties and sent her out to speak to Dorothy the receptionist.

As THE DOOR closed behind her, he put his head in his hands. This was so not going to work. How would he ever concentrate with her around? And living just across from him as well? She would be around him 24/7. He groaned. What was Jessie thinking of, sending him a girl like her? He had enough on his plate without that.

How had this happened in the space of a few hours? This morning he had been cool and calm; well, until he found Linda's car in his spot, when he'd suddenly exploded. And he knew why. He should never have gone to Nicola's parents in Glasgow last night to return the last of her belongings that he'd found in the apartment. They'd wined and dined him so well that he hadn't felt he could drive safely back home, and had booked into the first hotel he came across. Her parents had been so kind, and he could see they were disappointed that they had broken up. But they had, and no, he and Nicola weren't going to get together again, of that Andrew was determined. He'd had enough. Time to move on, but perhaps not as quickly as seemed to be the case with Jill on the scene.

But he urgently needed someone to pick up the slack now that Margery had taken leave to look after her family. And right in the middle of the Festival, too. It was his busiest time of year, and the time when he made new contacts, set up meetings, and brought interested parties together. His business depended on that.

Andrew decided that Jill would have to fill the gap left by Margery, and that work was the answer. Work, work, and more work. He'd give her so much work she'd be too tired to try any wiles on him. Not that plenty of work would be hard to find. There was more than enough to keep her busy, very busy.

She'd be so fed up with the sight of him that she'd ignore him if they did happen to meet on the stairs. He'd make it so she hated the sight of him. Damn it, he would not keep an eye on her as he'd promised Linda Naismith. Not even if she got herself into a right mess. He definitely would not let himself get involved with her.

He pressed the intercom. 'When you've finished explaining things to Miss Kennedy,' he told Dorothy, 'send her back in.'

THE DAY PASSED in a blur for Jill. She scribbled notes about everything he asked her to do. The main problem was a reception being held the next evening for various people associated with a Ukrainian ballet company who had been performing at the Festival and were heading home the day after. She had a list of names of caterers, wine suppliers, and florists, that she had to check through to see who was doing what, when, and where, as it wasn't the only event that Mr. Bossy was involved with.

'How am I going to sort all this out?' she wailed at Dorothy, as she flicked through the pages of notes. 'How can he expect me just to step in like that?'

Dorothy tapped her nose and slid across a piece of paper with a phone number written on it. 'Give Margery a ring,' she whispered.

'Who's Margery?' Jill whispered back, not sure why she was doing so.

'She's the PA you're replacing. Mr. MacCallum-Blair's given her compassionate leave as her daughter has had to go into hospital. She's six months pregnant and there are problems. So, Margery's looking after her two-year-old grandson. She won't mind you phoning. In fact, she told me to tell you to phone.'

A few moments later, Jill was sitting in Margery's office with the phone at her ear. It was ringing out.

'Come on, Margery,' Jill said, 'please answer. Don't be out in the park at the swings.'

Just as Jill was about to put the phone down, a rather breathless Margery answered.

'Sorry,' she said, after Jill explained who she was. 'I thought you might call. But I have to run so that I get to the phone before Donald. Otherwise, he picks it up and presses all the buttons and cuts the caller off. Anyway, I won this time and...' She broke off.

Jill heard her try to soothe a somewhat angry toddler who kept demanding, 'Me phone. Me phone.' His voice became more and more strident and eventually, Margery came back on the line. 'Can I phone you back in a few minutes? I think this calls for a trip to Granny's biscuit tin.'

Jill smiled to herself as she waited for the return call. It came surprisingly quickly.

'Thank goodness for homemade sultana scones,' Margery said. 'It takes him ages to pick out all the sultanas and eat them, so we've got at least… oh, five minutes.'

'Right,' said Jill, 'can you tell me…'

Before Donald had finished his snack, Margery had filled Jill in on all that needed to be done for the reception the next evening. 'It's all in that folder in the second drawer down. And don't hesitate to phone any time. Andrew is very particular, and likes to have everything organised and running like clockwork.'

'Oh dear,' said Jill, a worried tone creeping into her voice.

'Now don't you worry,' Margery said. 'He won't bite your head off. He's a lovely man to work for, and I'm sure he'll help you all he can.'

'Yeah, right,' Jill said sotto voce as she put the phone down. She was sure he'd be watching her closely, and at her first mistake, he'd be packing her off back to the employment agency with 'Useless' stamped on her file.

FORTUNATELY, Margery was obviously well organised, and everything was annotated in the file headed Ukrainian Ballet Reception in the second drawer down. It was simply a matter of phoning round the suppliers to check that they knew what and when to deliver the next day. Then, tomorrow afternoon, Jill would go to the hotel just off Princes Street where the event was being held, and oversee the setting up of the room and the buffet and drinks tables.

So, it was a very relieved Jill who cleared her desk at just after six in the evening and prepared to head down the stairs and home. Unfortunately, Mr. MacCallum-Blair had the same idea. She felt his eyes boring into her back as he followed her to the front door. But he marched ahead of her and pulled open the door. She stepped through, giving a short 'Goodnight' in reply to his, and watched as he ran down the steps and turned right.

She was just about to make her own way back home when a rumble of thunder presaged a torrent of rain from the dark grey clouds massing overhead. Jill groaned. She'd forgotten to bring an umbrella, and Linda's beautiful woolly jacket would be ruined if it got wet. Could she make it home before the rain really started? As if in answer, heavy black spots splattered onto the pavement.

She would have to make a dash for it. Jill held her handbag over her head, sprinted down the steps, turned left, and legged it along the street as fast as she could. There was no way she was able to match the speed of her prize-winning run in the under-17s 100 metres back at Coolundra High School, but she hoped she would at least get home before she was utterly soaked. She was just beginning to wish she had kept up her fitness levels when a car slowed alongside her.

She heard the whine of an electric window and a voice shouted across to her, 'Can I offer you a lift? After all, we are going the same way.'

Jill stopped and turned. It was all she could do to prevent herself telling him where he could put his lift, Linda's advice or not, but there was her aunt's jacket to consider. Reluctantly, she stepped across the road to the other side and opened the car door.

There was silence apart from the swish of the windscreen wipers and the occasional clicks of the indicators as Andrew drove. The car purred along the wet streets as the rain fell, creating minor tidal waves in the gutters which threatened to drench pedestrians unlucky enough to step too close to the curb. The only words spoken on the short trip back to the Canongate was the 'Thank you' she said when she climbed out. Mr. Bossy had merely nodded.

They silently ascended the stairs to their landing, Jill again intensely aware of his eyes on her bottom as he followed her. Bother him! She stuck the key in her lock, opened it first time, said 'Good night' and slammed the door.

'DAMN AND BLAST THE WOMAN!' Andrew swore as he closed his own door and leant against it. 'Damn and blast her! Why can't I just ignore her?'

He had intended to snub her outside of work, but the sight of her sprinting along the road, trying to keep the rain from her hair with her handbag, had meant that his inner good manners took over. And before he knew what he was doing, he'd slowed to her speed and opened the car window. He'd spent the whole journey berating himself for his foolishness, yet at the same time knowing he'd done the right thing in offering her a lift on such a terrible evening.

And if he admitted the truth, he was impressed by her running prowess, legs striding out, her hair streaming out behind her, and her face glowing from the exercise. She had looked so healthy and natural, so full of life, so everything that he admired in a woman. So tempting.

4

The reception was going well. Everything had gone very smoothly, and the food had been eagerly demolished by the troupe of ballet dancers and their entourage. And no wonder. Jill had been astounded at the range and quality of what was on offer.

'And all this is Scottish food?' she'd asked the chef as he oversaw the setting out of the buffet.

The tables were laden with all kinds of seafood; salmon, both fresh and smoked, trout, crab, langoustines, oysters, scallops and prawns, temptingly displayed amongst beds of fresh salad leaves or in heated tableware. Further on, the chef pointed out venison and pheasant dishes, as well as roast beef and lamb. 'All sourced in Scotland and bought fresh and organic, if possible,' he told her. 'We have it all on our doorstep. Proper food. There's not a haggis or mutton pie or deep-fried Mars bar anywhere.'

'Oh, the desserts are to die for!' Jill exclaimed as helpers brought in trays of glorious puddings. 'What is that?' she asked as a particularly tasty one was set out.

'Cranachan,' said the chef, whose name was Ian.

'Raspberries, cream, whisky, and honey. And that one's Atholl Brose. Oatmeal steeped overnight and then honey and whisky are added. Delicious!'

'And intoxicating!' said Jill.

'Ah well, we need something to keep out the cold and the rain.'

The room took on a warming glow despite its grand proportions and décor. Tall windows ranged across one side, flanked by long, dark red velvet curtains swooping to the floor. The carpet was a red and green tartan which would have overwhelmed a lesser room, but in this one it seemed to blend in exactly. Chandeliers hung at intervals from the ceiling, decorated as Jill noticed, in a style not dissimilar to that of Andrew's office. The whole effect was gracious and welcoming, and well-nigh perfect to her eyes.

There was a long bar just inside the door and several shelves were filled with quality single malts and blends. Jill had no doubt they were the best whiskies that Scotland had to offer. Mr. Bossy always wanted the best.

'And I want a drink,' she said out loud as she approached the bar. 'What do you suggest?'

'Whisky, of course,' said the black waist-coated barman. 'What about a wee taste of this one? It's a beautiful pale blend and not too strong for a lady. I think you'll like it.'

He poured out a generous measure in a small glass and handed it to her.

'Could you put a spot of ginger in it, please?' Jill asked.

The barman looked stunned. 'You're not going to spoil a good whisky by putting that rubbish in it?' he said. 'A spot of water, if you must, but it's far better neat.'

'I'm sorry,' she said. She could see that he was horrified at her request, so she took the glass of neat whisky and raised it to him before taking a tentative sip. The liquid flowed down her throat and a warm afterglow suffused her mouth.

'Hey,' she said, 'that is just… just fantastic!'

The barman nodded. 'That's the way you're supposed to drink it, not full of that stuff you wanted.'

She left him to his grumbles and surveyed the room. If Andrew MacCallum-Blair wasn't pleased with the arrangements, then she was blowed if anything would please him.

And now she could relax a little and mingle with the guests. The Lord Provost was there, her gold chain glinting in the lights and her hearty laugh booming above the rest of the conversations. Andrew moved graciously among the guests, exchanging a word here, a pat on the back there. He was now deep in conversation with one of the principal ballet dancers – a tiny slip of a woman who, Jill was surprised to notice, was not exactly in the first flush of youth. Yet, the reviews had praised her for her dancing and the passion she exuded; in fact, the troupe had been one of the highlights of the Festival, and had been sold out many months before. It was obviously a great coup for Andrew to be hosting the reception for them.

'You are not Scottish then, Jill?' The Ukrainian accent sounded to Jill like something from a James Bond film. She smiled up at the tall, well-muscled young man with the mischievous grin and the fair hair flopping over his eyes.

'No, I'm from Australia. I'm over here for several months to travel around and see something of the country.' She had to raise her voice over the clink of glasses and general hum of conversation.

'You perhaps will visit my country then?' The Ukrainian drew her attention back to him.

'I'd love to,' Jill smiled. 'Though I don't know if my money will stretch that far.'

'You will stay with me,' he said. 'I will show you my

country, and we will get to know each other so much better, no?'

'That sounds lovely,' Jill said, 'but I don't think I'll manage to come this year. Perhaps some other time. Maybe your company will come to Australia to perform?'

The Ukrainian's face lit up. 'You will ask that we come? I like to see Australia very much. All beautiful girls in bikinis on beaches, yes?'

'Yes, well, I'll see what I can do.' Maybe she had a career ahead of her as an events organiser if the success of this one was anything to go by.

'And you are interested in the ballet?' His blue eyes were large and staring right into hers.

'I don't know very much about it.' She wasn't going to admit that the only ballet she'd ever seen was on TV, and that as a child, she'd eschewed ballet lessons in favour of tennis coaching. 'Are you one of the dancers?'

'Yes, I am Grigor Lutsenko. I am principal male dancer.'

Crikes! That blew her cover. Now Jill realised that he would know she knew nothing about ballet, and worse, hadn't even seen one of the troupe's performances. 'I've only just arrived over here. I haven't had a chance to see much of the Festival.'

'I am sorry that you not see me dance. I think that you would like me.'

'I like you very much already,' Jill said, raising her glass of whisky to him. 'What a pity you're leaving tomorrow.'

They shared a smile. 'A great pity,' he purred. 'What is it that you do? For work, I mean?'

'I work for Andrew MacCallum-Blair, you know, the guy who's organised this bash.'

'This what you say?'

'Bash. Get-together. Reception.'

'Ah yes.' The puzzled look on Grigor's face was replaced by that enchanting grin. 'This Andrew, he is your boss?'

'Yes, there he is over there.' She raised her hand to point to him through the crowd just in time to see Andrew glare back at her. Oh dear, what was she doing that he didn't like?

Grigor caught the look, too. 'He is not pleased that you talk to me,' he said. 'He is your lover?'

'Certainly not!' The words exploded from Jill. She would have said more but bit her tongue just in time.

'That is good,' said Grigor. 'Then perhaps you like to be my lover? We have tonight, you know. I don't leave till eleven hundred hours tomorrow. We have good evening together, and I show you the Ukrainian way of make love.'

'Thank you, Grigor,' Jill answered, trying not to blush or giggle. He certainly didn't believe in wasting time. 'Another time perhaps. When I come to the Ukraine.' Not that she had any intention of so doing, but she was trying to let him down as gracefully as she could.

'Everything going ok?' Suddenly, Andrew was standing beside her. She hadn't noticed his approach. A shiver tingled its way down her spine and settled in her stomach, where it transformed itself into butterflies playing leapfrog.

'Yes, fine.' She gripped her whisky glass more tightly to stop her hand from trembling. At that moment, one of Edinburgh's finest dowager ladies hooked her hand through Grigor's arm and led him off to another group. Grigor turned as she dragged him away and shrugged his shoulders at Jill. Another time, another place was the message she took from the gesture.

She smiled, and smiled even more broadly when she took in that Andrew had noticed Grigor's shrug and now had a deep frown across his brow. Oh, let him be an old fuddy-duddy, she thought. Another reason for telling her off. Fraternising with the guests. No doubt he was about to list all her faults and omissions for this evening before telling her that her services were no longer required.

She decided to pre-empt him. 'How did you feel the evening has gone?' she said in as silky a tone as she could muster.

He cleared his throat and looked at the tartan carpet. 'Actually, very well,' he said. 'I must say, you've done a great job.'

Jill was taken aback. He was actually praising her. Although he couldn't look her straight in the eye when telling her so, but he definitely was having to say nice things about her organisation of the event.

'Yes,' he went on, 'it's all gone very smoothly, and everybody has said how good the food was. The whisky tasting went down well, too.' He paused again and studied the carpet, and then looked up at the ceiling. 'But of course, most of the organising was done by Margery, so really all you had to do was make sure it all ran to schedule. The real test will come next week.' This time, he looked straight at Jill. 'I've decided we will organise a party for the last night of the Festival. I'll give you a guest list, and tomorrow morning you can get on with arranging it.'

Andrew let a half smile flicker across his lips before he turned away and joined a group where the Lord Provost was detailing the new tram system to some less than enthralled guests.

'What a whinger!' Jill said under her breath. 'It nearly choked him to tell me that I'd done a good job.' And he'd set her another, far more difficult test. Well, more fool him, he wasn't getting rid of her as easily as that. First thing tomorrow morning, she'd be back on the phone to Margery.

. . .

By the time the last guest had meandered their way towards the exit, it was almost dark; not that summer evenings in Edinburgh ever get completely dark for long. And it was dry. Jill decided to walk, as she felt the need of some fresh air and some time to come down after such an adrenalin rush of a day. She avoided the shorter but darker and quieter route home, via one of Edinburgh's many closes – narrow alleyways linking the Royal Mile to streets on either side of it – and instead stuck to the main road across the North Bridge. A soft breeze was blowing which ruffled her hair.

On an impulse, she pulled out the clasps holding it in a loose chignon and let it fall to her shoulders. She felt at ease with herself and pleased and happy with the evening's success. Grigor's attentions had boosted her confidence and brought a smile to her features. It was nice to be propositioned by such a handsome young man. The image of his tightly muscled body came back to her, and she sighed. A night with him would have been something to tell the grandchildren about. Or maybe not. She wouldn't want to shock them.

A passing merry drunk brought her back to the present. He had nearly bumped into her as he wended his way, and Jill realised she should be more aware of her surroundings. Her heart gave an extra thump when she saw just ahead of her the hotel where the Ukrainian Ballet Company were staying. It was an old sandstone building, converted from a former bank into a luxury hotel, and now filled with ballet dancers including Grigor. She paused outside the revolving doors at the entrance and looked in at the brightly lit interior. She could just walk in, give her name at the desk, and ask for Mr. Lutsenko's room number. It was as simple as that. Or as difficult. What if he had already found somebody else to spend the night with? She couldn't imagine him being short of women all too willing to sleep with him.

She would probably be only one of many. He probably wouldn't even remember her name in the morning. But she would remember his. A night spent in the arms of Grigor Lutsenko was sure to be memorable. Again, her imagination took over and she envisioned his rippling torso leaning over her and his arms encircling her body. She tingled. What wouldn't she give for an experience like that? In your dreams, she told herself firmly, and walked on.

5

Diagonally across the road from the hotel, a sleek black car was stopped on double yellow lines with its engine still running. Andrew sat behind the wheel, his hands clenched into fists as he watched Jill outside the hotel. Surely she wasn't going to go to that dancer who had been chatting her up at the reception? She'd been enjoying his advances, he had seen her face light up when she spoke to the Ukrainian and her body seemed to soften and relax in his company. Yet, she had always seemed so rigid and tense when he was around. And he supposed, that was all his fault. He couldn't relax in front of her. She made him too impatient for the niceties of socialising, he wanted to taste her lips, to run his hands over her breasts, to... He put his hands over his face and sighed.

When he looked up again, he couldn't see Jill. She had disappeared. There was a crowd of people standing outside the entrance to the hotel, trying to find an empty taxi to hail. But where was Jill? Had she actually gone into the hotel? Was she even now in the lift on her way up to the dancer's room? Surely she wouldn't share his bed for the night? But he was sure that that was exactly what was going through her mind. What normal, healthy, single woman wouldn't want to experience sex with such a man?

And what business was it of his who she slept with? Why was he so concerned about whether or not she was heading for the bed of a ballet dancer? Because, he had to admit to himself, he wanted to be the one whose bed she shared. He wanted it to be him that she swooned over, that she craved, that she slipped into bed with.

A taxi eventually stopped and the laughing group surged into it, leaving behind an empty pavement. There was so sign of Jill anywhere. Had she gone into the hotel or was she walking back to the flat? Gritting his teeth in frustration, Andrew put the car into gear and headed home. He was not going to torture himself thinking about what she might or might not be doing. He was tired and had another busy day ahead of him. He'd better get a good night's sleep before he had to face the prospect of working closely with Jill, suspecting all the while that she had another man's scent on her.

He ran up the stairs to his flat and slammed the door shut, not caring if he disturbed the other residents.

Get to bed, he kept telling himself. You don't care where she is. It's none of your business. Put her out of your head. There are more important things. You are not going to get involved with another woman just yet.

As he went into his bedroom, he heard footsteps coming up the spiral stairs. He stepped out into his hallway and moved quietly towards the outside door. The footsteps kept coming. Were they going to stop outside Jill's flat, or would they move on up to the flats above them? He couldn't tell whether they were made by a man or a woman, but there was definitely only one person. If it was Jill, then she was alone. She wouldn't be with

Grigor whatever his name was or anyone else for that matter.

He listened, holding his breath as the footsteps came closer, closer. They stopped. Then he heard a key ratcheting around in a lock and, eventually, the door across from his opened. Jill. He heard it shut and the door chain being rattled into place. She was back. A long, low sigh came from him as he exhaled and began to breathe normally again.

He glanced at his watch. Only minutes had passed since he'd been watching her outside the hotel, only enough time for her to walk home. To walk home. Not to go into the hotel and meet up with that… that… He forced a grim smile. Why was he thinking so unkindly of that dancer? The guy was probably happily tucked up in bed with one of the other dancers. There were no doubt plenty to choose from.

Feeling the tension at last releasing itself from his body, he made ready for bed. But when he eventually got settled, Andrew found sleep wasn't forthcoming. After tossing and turning for what seemed like hours, he threw aside his duvet and padded through to the lounge and his laptop.

Thoughts about his new PA had been besieging him all that time. He would find out more about her, what she was like, her background, who her family were, and of course the best person to ask was Linda Naismith. She'd left him her email address so that he could contact her about any problems relating to the property, like burst pipes, or stair cleaning, or communal roof repairs, all the minutiae of communal life in an old tenement building.

He sent an email zinging through the ether.

ACROSS THE LANDING, Jill felt unready for sleep. Her brain

was going over the events of the evening, as she was still far too wide awake for bed. Instead, she switched on Linda's computer and decided to email her about her new job, and perhaps find out a bit more about her bossy boss.

Why was it everybody else seemed to think that Andrew MacCallum-Blair was such a nice guy, when all she seemed to receive from him was aggro and back-handed compliments when he was forced to be nice to her? What had she done to him that made him so bad-tempered whenever she was around? Was it really all because she had parked in his space? Was he really so anal about things like that?

The computer hummed into life, and Jill's fingers flew across the keyboard as she told Linda all about the happenings of the last two hectic days.

IN AUSTRALIA, Linda ordered an Americano coffee and settled herself in front of a screen in an Internet café. When she accessed her emails, a broad smile spread over her face. This was looking interesting. Things were happening, though not quite in the way she had anticipated.

Now, what was the best way to tackle it and help things along? She took a sip of her coffee and thought.

6

The next few days seemed to blur together for Jill. Every morning there was a long list of things to do scrawled over a piece of paper and left on her desk. But of Andrew she saw very little. Which was just as well, as she spent quite a lot of time on the phone to Margery. She got to know young Donald's routine very well, and made a point of phoning when she was pretty sure he was having his afternoon nap, or enjoying his elevenses, or at the mother and toddler group. She became used to conversations about Australian versus South African wines, which Margery was keen on buying in, punctuated with snatches of Postman Pat or Incy Wincy Spider.

She'd also arranged a coded signal from Dorothy to let her know when Andrew was about, so that he wouldn't catch her picking Margery's brains. She wanted him to think that the arranging was all her own work. But he seemed to spend most of his days out and about, only coming into the office to check with Dorothy about appointments and phone calls. Jill, he ignored apart from a curt good morning, or a nod if she was on the phone to a caterer or wine merchant, or trying to pretend it wasn't Margery on the end of the line.

'Just say, "Mr. MacCallum-Blair would like that" and I'll know you can't talk and I'll ring off,' suggested Margery. 'You can phone back when he's gone.'

When she did have a few minutes to herself, she found her thoughts slipping back to Grigor Lutsenko and his finely tuned, elegantly proportioned body. He would be safely back in the Ukraine now, so she felt free to ponder over what might have been if only she'd had the courage to say 'yes' to his proposition. A night to explore his athleticism, his masculinity, his grace, his libido, would have been a night never to be forgotten, a night of nights, a night by which every other man would be compared and probably rejected.

But would he have remembered her? Probably not. She would be exactly where she was at the moment, organising a party for various performers at the Fringe – an offshoot of the official Festival, with even more shows and performers. She was looking forward to meeting some of them, as the Fringe was a favourite place for up-and-coming stars to try out their acts, as well as for established performers keen to hone their stand-up skills or to act in new and cutting-edge drama. With Andrew's contacts, the guest list was like a who's who of current big names and ones to watch.

'Can you do this for me, please?' Andrew's voice broke into her thoughts and Jill started guiltily. What would her boss think if he knew she had been daydreaming about handsome, leonine dancers?

'Can you go to this show tonight and speak to the singer?' Andrew said, handing Jill a ticket. 'Apparently, he's extremely good, and I think it would be great for him to meet with some of the agents and impresarios coming to the party.'

'Who is it?' she asked.

'Sam O'Connor. He's Irish and has done quite well there, but now he's looking to break into the UK scene. This is his first gig over here, and every night's been a sell-out.'

Jill had been looking forward to a quiet night in washing her hair, giving herself a manicure as her nails had been given a battering opening files and working on the computer, and generally catching up with her emails from friends and family. She decided that that would have to be shelved.

As Andrew explained where the venue was, she worked out that she would just have time to grab a bite to eat after leaving the office, before making her way to the Cowgate.

'Why is it called the Cowgate?' Jill asked. 'Were there cows there?'

Andrew smiled. 'Yes, the cows were herded along it on their way to market. Gate means "street" in Scots. Like Canongate where we live.'

'So, Canongate means where... where canons lived?'

'Yes, they were Augustinian canons who were granted their own parish there in the twelfth century.'

'The twelfth century?' Jill expressed astonishment. 'Geez, Australia's only been going since the eighteenth.'

'For the white man, perhaps. But your Aborigines have been living there since well before the twelfth century.'

'Touché,' Jill said with a wry smile. This man really knew his history. But living in a place like Edinburgh, where you were surrounded by centuries of the stuff, how could anyone not fail to absorb it in their pores? They probably sucked it in their mother's milk.

'So, I go to this place in the Cowgate,' said Jill getting

back to the ticket she was holding in her hand, 'watch this guy, and then what?'

'If you think he's as good as he's claimed to be, then catch him after the show and give him an invitation. You'll need to sell it to him, point out how advantageous it could be for him to meet with some of my other guests.'

'You trust my judgement?'

Andrew didn't hesitate at her question. 'Of course.' He looked straight into her eyes. 'I think you have very good taste.' Especially in men, he thought, conjuring up an image of a certain Ukrainian.

Once the Festival was over, he decided, he would spend more time out jogging, walking the hills, getting himself back to a level of fitness. Although it would be nothing like as supreme as Grigor Lutsenko's, he hoped it would bring back the six-pack he had been so proud of not so long ago. Before I got into running the business, he thought. Since then, I haven't had a moment to myself. But he knew that had been deliberate. He hadn't wanted to have any spare moments to think about the past and what might have been. Rather, he'd put his head down, and worked and worked. It was his way of coping, of waiting for healing time to do its work, and stitch over the raw wounds he'd been left with.

Now though, he felt ridiculously alive and aware of the gaps in his life, gaps that Jill seemed unconsciously to remind him of. The lack of a special someone, of someone he could laugh with and tell inner thoughts to, to have a shared private language and shorthand ways of communicating, to have a warm, familiar body to wake up beside in the mornings. To want to stay in bed, and not have to throw himself out of it and into work at some ridiculous time every morning.

He watched her as she perused the ticket in her hand.

Was she going to refuse to go, claiming some prior arrangement?

'Okay.' Her luminescent green eyes met his. 'But could I come in later tomorrow to make up for it? I think everything's under control. I can catch up with any problems in the afternoon.'

Andrew's eyes flamed. 'You *think* everything's under control? Either it is, or it isn't. If it's not, then I expect you here by nine am at the latest. I want everything to be perfect, do you understand? Second best isn't good enough.'

With that, he turned on his heel, strode into his office, and slammed the door.

Jill's mouth fell open. What on earth had caused that outburst? Dorothy caught her eye, and threw up her hands in dumbfounded shock. Silently, they both settled back down to work. Jill sighed. If perfection was what he wanted, then she'd give him it. Nothing would be left to chance. She'd double and triple check every last detail until she saw it in her dreams; nightmares more like it.

So, if her hair looked like tumbleweed and she was wearing the same blouse several days on the trot, then that was his problem. She couldn't do everything.

As soon as she heard him stomping down the stairs and the front door banging, she rang Margery. Donald was fortunately engrossed with a video and almost ready for a nap.

'Oh dear, that's so unlike him,' Margery said. 'Poor lamb, he must be under a lot of stress.'

Poor lamb indeed. That was not quite how Jill would have described him, more like a wolf in the proverbial sheep's clothing.

'It sounds like he really needs a break,' Margery went on. 'He hasn't had a proper holiday for yonks, not since…

well, I won't say anything about that, but he definitely needs a break.'

Unable to take any more of Margery's sympathy for her boss, Jill made her excuses and rang off. She shuffled the papers on her desk and set about rearranging her schedule to take in the concert that evening.

7

'Maney your gods be always sitting on your shoulder,
and your pockets be filled with luck. Thank you,
ladies and gentlemen, and goodnight.'

Jill joined in with the fulsome applause. Sam O'Connor
had been brilliant. His songs had, in turn, been funny and
heart-warming, poignant and stirring. Some were his own,
others from Ireland's cornucopia of music. His voice was
warm and soulful, in places untrained and rough and
ready, but always with his heart in his music. And in
between, his tales of a childhood spent in some of the
more out-of-the-way parts of the Republic as part of an
ever-expanding and poor family, were hilarious and sad,
heart-breaking and life-affirming, comic and tragic, all in
the same breath. Jill found herself alternately laughing and
crying, so much so that in the end she was never quite sure
which one it was.

He had seemed at first to be dwarfed by the stage, but
as he warmed to his task, he metaphorically grew until his
presence filled the theatre and spilled out over the audience. They cheered and encored him, calling him back for

one more song, another story, until he held up his hands and asked, 'Do you folk not have homes to go to? Has the last bus not gone yet?'

Jill struggled through the crowd, pushing her way towards the stage as the audience made for the exits. By the time she reached it, Sam had disappeared. She was just about to climb onto the stage when a hand reached out to stop her.

'Sorry, you're not allowed. The exit's over there.'

'But I need to speak to Sam,' she explained to the security guy. 'I have an invitation for him.'

The man smirked. 'Not another one. If I had a pound for every invitation he's received from beautiful young women, I'd be as wealthy as Trump.'

Jill bristled. 'It's from my boss,' she said. 'An invitation to meet with some agents and impresarios. It could be the break he's waiting for.'

'I've heard that one, too,' the man said. 'I must say, you lot are inventive when it comes to making up stories to twist my arm with. "I was at school with him and he wrote me a song." "My mother and his mother were best friends." "We met when he did a gig in New York." As we Scots say, aye right!'

Jill tried to look as formal and serious as she could, thankful that she was still wearing her office clothes. She began again. 'My boss is Andrew MacCallum-Blair, and he sent me along this evening to assess Sam's potential and to issue an invitation to a party Andrew's having to meet with some showbiz friends of his. I would be grateful if you could direct me to his dressing-room.'

The security man laughed, and leaning forward into Jill's face, said, 'Prove it.'

Jill leant forward until her nose almost touched his and said, 'I will.'

With a last haughty glare at him, she rummaged in her handbag and brought out Andrew's invitation. The man took it and carefully read every word, before turning it over and scrutinising the blank back.

He handed it back to her with a wry smile. 'You win. Come on.'

Jill followed him down a dingy corridor to a door at the end. Without even knocking, the security man opened it and ushered Jill in. It was nothing more than a broom cupboard containing a mirror, a chair with a couple of clothes hangers hooked over the back, and a small table on which Sam was sitting strumming his guitar.

'Someone important to see you,' the man said with a wink to Sam. 'Don't be long. I'm locking up in half an hour.'

Jill held out her hand. 'I'm Jill Kennedy, Andrew MacCallum-Blair's PA. I'm here to invite you to a party he's giving for Fringe performers.'

Sam's warm hand took hers and he grinned. 'I'm pleased to meet you, Jill Kennedy. Now, when would the party be?' His Irish voice had a lilt to it, not unlike the Scots accents, but Jill was now so attuned to them that she could distinguish the different cadences in his voice.

He was as easy to talk to as his songs were to listen to, and before Jill knew what was happening, she was sitting in an Irish pub nearby with a long glass of some dark brown beer in front of her and laughter and music all around. Irish accents mingled with Scots voices and, as well as her own Australian tones, there were a couple of North American ones. But whether they were Canadian or American, she never got close enough to find out.

Sam sang some songs to great applause, and was followed by other singers who encouraged everyone to join in the choruses of what appeared to be Irish and Scottish folk tunes, well known to the audience but new to Jill. A group of Japanese tourists were sitting clutching glasses of whisky, looking suitably puzzled but enthralled at the proceedings. It must seem like some ancient fertility rite to them, Jill thought, as a barmaid laden with a tray of beers, skilfully manoeuvred her way between the tables.

Jill knew only that it was late, very late, when the taxi she had shared with Sam dropped her off outside her flat.

'See you at the party then, me darling,' Sam slurred softly as Jill clambered out. 'Goodnight to you, then.'

'Goodnight Sam,' Jill said before she shut the door and the taxi purred away.

Wearily, she climbed the stairs to her flat. If Mr. Bossy wanted her in the office by nine am, she was not going to get much beauty sleep. In fact, two or three hours at the most. And she still hadn't washed her hair. Or done her nails. Or emailed all the people she'd meant to.

ACROSS THE LANDING, Andrew woke from the light doze he'd drifted into. Someone was climbing the stairs. Was it Jill? He squinted at his clock.

'Three forty-six. Where the hell has she been till this time? The show finished at around eleven.'

He listened and heard the familiar ratcheting as Jill battled with the lock. Well, he'd make sure she was in the office at the usual time. If she was going to play hard, then he would ensure that she worked hard, too.

8

Jill surfaced through a long tunnel. Bells were ringing; an insistent one, and one that pierced her brain, sending shafts of pain through her head. She dragged herself awake and reached over to the bedside table. Fumbling around, she found her alarm clock and switched it off. Eight o'clock. What had possessed her to set it for then? Then she remembered. Work. Mr. Bossy wanted her in the office for nine.

She was just about to snuggle down again for a quick five minutes when the other bell from her dreams shrilled. Jill jumped. The doorbell! Who could be ringing her doorbell at this time? She flung on Linda's woolly dressing-gown, which she'd resurrected from the wardrobe, and padded down the hall to the front door. To be safe, she squinted through the spy-hole to see who it was. She groaned. What on earth did he want?

She opened the door to Andrew, aware of her ruffled hair, of the makeup she hadn't been bothered to remove when she went to bed, of Linda's comfy but somewhat moth-eaten robe.

'I was going to offer to give you a lift into work,' Andrew said, a smile flickering over his face. 'It looks as if it might rain. But I can see you're not quite ready.'

'It's eight o'clock,' Jill said in as haughty a tone as she could muster. 'I don't start work till nine. I shall be there then.'

With that, she shut the door and called Mr. Bossy every Australian insult she could think of. Then she threw off the dressing-gown, charged into the bathroom, and turned on the shower.

At one minute to nine, Jill climbed the stairs to the office. She said good morning to Dorothy who was just taking off her coat, and nodded briefly to Andrew who was speaking on the phone in his office, the door of which stood open. No doubt to catch me sneaking in late, Jill thought. But she wasn't. She went into her own office, closed the door, and high-fived the air. One up to her.

Then she sat down to catch her breath. It had been one hell of a rush, showering, washing and drying her hair, repairing the ravage to her face, swallowing some break-fast, then sprinting down The Mound and across Princes Street, dodging pedestrians and early morning tour buses in her attempt to reach Andrew's office in time. But she'd made it. Not that she felt great. To be quite honest she didn't, but her early morning jog had chased away some of her cobwebs and she felt better than she expected or deserved to.

She quietly opened her door, checked that Andrew's was now closed, and signalled 'coffee' to Dorothy. Dorothy grinned and got up. A few moments later, a steaming hot, very strong coffee was sitting on her desk. She would run on caffeine today and catch up on her sleep tonight.

Somehow, she survived the day, only the spell after lunch threatening to defeat her. All she wanted to do was put her head on the desk and close her eyes, but Andrew hadn't been out of the office all day and she knew she didn't dare risk it. So, at five on the dot, she cleared her desk, helped Dorothy on with her coat, and the two of them walked down the stairs together.

'I'm having an early night,' she told Dorothy. 'Nine o'clock at the latest.'

'I thought you young things had all the energy in the world,' Dorothy said. 'Look at Andrew. He's always on the go. Though he has been looking tired lately. It's all the Festival organisation and entertaining he has to do.'

Jill said nothing. Another fan of Andrew. They parted at the corner of the street and Jill headed home.

Before she had her early night, Jill made herself open up her email account and start replying to the messages she'd received. She wrote a long one to her mum, and several to friends from university. Feeling very pleased with herself, she was about to close it when another email pinged into her box. It was from Linda.

After a long account of where she'd been, and what she'd seen and eaten and bought, her aunt added,

I know that Andrew wants to take you to the Tattoo at the Castle. It's the highlight of the Festival and well worth seeing. Mind you wrap up warm and buy one of the rain ponchos they sell on the street. I know you'll enjoy it, and Andrew will tell you all about the castle and its history. He knows so much about Edinburgh.

Fat chance of that happening, Jill thought. There was no way she and her boss were going to spend an evening together, even though she was dying to see the Tattoo. Tickets had sold out weeks ago, and for now she had to content herself with the sound of the pipes and drums reverberating from the castle down the Royal Mile to the Canongate. That, and occasional glimpses of the firework finale above the rooftops.

She got ready for bed, and by half past nine was sound asleep. She didn't hear Andrew climbing the stairs and pause outside her door for a moment before going into his flat. He, too, went to his computer to check his emails. He, too, had one from Linda. He, too, had a long account of her travels before reading,

Jill would love to see the Tattoo. Do you think you could take her? I know with all your connections you should be able to drum up a couple of tickets from somewhere. It would so make her stay in the city memorable.

'Linda Naismith,' Andrew said aloud. 'You are a scheming, plotting, conniving, manipulative woman. I would love to read what you've said to Jill.'

9

Rain was blowing into their faces as Jill and Andrew made their way up Castle Hill to the Esplanade at Edinburgh Castle for the Tattoo. Andrew was carrying a tartan rug in deep blues and purples, while Jill carried two rain ponchos Andrew had purchased from a street seller.

'I think we're going to need these soon,' she said, as she struggled against the strong gusts of wind battering heavy raindrops into their faces.

'What? This is just a normal summer's evening here,' Andrew grinned. 'Don't tell me you're chickening out.'

'No chance,' she replied, and she meant it. She still couldn't quite believe that she was doing this. When Andrew had come into her office that morning with what she could only describe as a sheepish look on his face, and asked if she would like to go to the Tattoo with him, she had surprised herself by enthusiastically accepting. What was she thinking of? She had been so adamant that there was no way she would do such a thing, yet she hadn't even hesitated. What was it about this man that made her behave like that? And was Linda psychic? How did she know that Andrew was going to ask her? Were they in touch? Surely Linda would have mentioned if she had heard from him?

And here they were, making their way along with the hundreds of other people who were part of that night's audience, up the steep Castle Hill. As the road narrowed, their pace slowed, and they were offered some protection from the weather by the huddled masses. At last, they found their way to their seats on the steep banking of metal scaffolding ranged either side of the esplanade, in front of the castle's entrance over the moat.

Andrew spread the rug over their knees while Jill unpacked the ponchos, and each pulled one over their heads. People on either side of them were doing the same, and before long the entire audience looked like a collection of bright yellow and blue gnomes perched on garden centre display units, with only the odd flash of red or green to break the pattern.

'I'm glad you brought the rug,' Jill said, as a chilly blast of night air swept across the area. She tucked her hands under the edge of the cosy but light rug, and suddenly became aware of the warmth emanating from Andrew's thigh which was almost touching hers. She gasped, and he looked at her, surprised.

'Are you all right? Are you comfortable enough?'

'Yes, I'm fine,' she said, suddenly all too conscious of the effect his proximity was having on her. She attempted to concentrate instead on what was happening around her, and was glad when the floodlights illuminating the castle gradually faded. For a brief moment, there was total darkness before the sound of the massed pipe bands heralded the start of the Edinburgh Military Tattoo.

More and more pipers poured out of the narrow entrance to the castle, and spread out across the esplanade.

They marched in formation, all the while playing a variety of tunes, many of which seemed to Jill to imitate the lilt of the soft Scottish accents she was becoming attuned to. Then followed dancers from Cambodia, acrobats and jugglers from China, American school marching bands, African Zulu warriors, all colourful and exotic, and superb performers.

Jill forgot all about the rain and the wind as she watched, though every so often, when she craned her body to see a particularly spectacular performer, her leg nudged Andrew's and a jolt like electricity shot through her body. Apart from exclamations at what they were watching, and occasional nods and smiles of appreciation, Jill and Andrew didn't talk, simply soaking up the magnificence of the display and the precision and accuracy of the dancers and entertainers.

At the finale, every performer entered the stage area and the massed bands struck up once more. The *Evening Hymn* was played, and the audience joined in the singing. Jill heard Andrew's fine baritone voice next to her and she leaned closer to enjoy his voice. Then the *Last Post* sounded and the flags were lowered. As the last notes died away, the lights dimmed, and far away on the utmost parapet of the castle, a lone piper played a haunting melody that brought tears to Jill's eyes.

Then all was dark until, in an explosion of colour and noise, fireworks burst over the castle. To finish, the bands struck up *Auld Lang Syne*, and the audience rose, joined hands, and sang lustily,

Should auld acquaintance be forgot and never brought to min'.
Should auld acquaintance be forgot for the sake of auld lang syne.

Andrew took Jill's hand in his, but she was unaware who held her other, and they swung hands and sang while her heart thumped in time to the music. When, at the last verse, they crossed their arms to link with the person next to them, Jill found herself drawn closely to Andrew's side. And the fireworks that shot through her at his touch, were far more explosive than the ones they had just watched.

She took his arm as they made their way down the wet cobbles of Castle Hill to their building. The rain was still beating down and, although the ponchos gave them some protection, Jill could feel her jeans getting damper by the minute. She was glad she'd worn her trainers, as the street was slippy underfoot and they were going as fast as they could to get out of the rain.

By the time they reached their building and pushed open the main door, Jill's hair had darkened with the rain and her face glowed from the wind. Rain ran down Andrew's face and dripped from his poncho, leaving a damp trail as they climbed the stairs.

'A change of clothing and some hot chocolate is called for,' he said. 'I'll put the kettle on while you get changed. Just come through when you're ready. I'll leave the door on the latch.'

'Thanks,' said Jill. 'That sounds great.' For once, she opened her flat door without any bother and went into her bedroom. Well, she thought, times they are a-changing. A night out with Mr. Bossy and an invitation for hot chocolate in his flat.

Slipping off her trainers, she grabbed a towel and rubbed at her hair, then stripped off her wet jeans and socks. Scottish rain is really penetrating, she thought, as she wiped the dampness from her legs.

Jill pulled on a pair of jogging trousers and cosied her feet into a pair of sheepskin slippers that Linda had left. A quick brush of her hair, and she was ready. She didn't even bother looking in the mirror before she left, but pulled her door closed and walked across the landing to Andrew's flat.

As promised, the door was open and she went in, calling 'hello' as she did so. There was an answering shout from the kitchen.

Jill stood in his hallway to get her bearings. The flat was identical to Linda's except in mirror image. But its style was worlds apart. Whereas Linda's was stuffed with belongings and strewn with knick-knacks, Andrew's was minimalist and modern and tidy. At that moment, he came out of the kitchen carrying two steaming mugs of hot chocolate.

'Come into the lounge,' he said.

Jill followed him into what was the bedroom in Linda's flat. To Jill's surprise it seemed so much bigger and airier. Two cream leather sofas sat on either side of what must have been the original fireplace, with its marble mantelpiece, while a widescreen and up-to-the-minute television stood in a corner.

'This is lovely,' she said, 'and so different.'

'From Linda's? That wouldn't be hard. I've never known anyone with so much clutter. She's a hoarder. She could open her own shop; she's got enough clothes and accessories.'

'She's got some nice things, though.' Linda defended her aunt.

'If you could see them. I see you found her nice cashmere jacket that you wore to the office and...' he looked down at her feet, '...her slippers.'

'I'm sure she won't mind my borrowing them,' Jill replied, a firm note entering her voice. 'She can borrow my clothes while she's in Oz. I don't mind.'

Andrew grinned. 'I'd love to see that. Linda Naismith in one of your bikinis!'

'She'd look pretty good in them. You're never too old for a bikini at the beach.'

Their voices were becoming raised. They paused, and Andrew pushed a cup across the coffee table to Jill.

'Pax,' he said. 'Drink up and warm yourself. I'll put the fire on for you. It was pretty cold out there tonight.'

Bending down, he pressed a switch, and immediately flames burned in the hearth.

'I thought it was a real fireplace,' said Jill, somewhat disappointed.

'It is,' he said, 'but brought up to date. There's no way I'm carrying coal up two flights of stairs and then mucking about with sticks and paper. This is simple and easy, and it looks like the real thing even though it's gas.'

'Has Linda's room still got the fireplace, too?'

Andrew nodded. 'I think it's behind the bed-head, but you can't see it. She claims she prefers sleeping at the front, but this room is supposed to be the lounge so I kept it that way.'

A sudden thought struck Jill. 'How well do you know Linda?' she asked.

Andrew laughed. 'The first day I moved in here, she came across with a bowl of homemade Scotch broth for me. We've been firm friends ever since. We're not alike in our tastes, she's a bit older than me and we argue the whole time, but she's great fun. And her parties are something else.' He shook his head. 'Boy, the nights we've had. All the neighbours come so that no-one complains about the noise, and every other interesting character that's in town is there. Sometimes it's been dawn before we've got to our beds. She's a real party animal is your auntie.'

This side of her aunt was new to Jill. She wondered how her mum was getting on with the sister she hadn't seen for many years. Or perhaps Mum was joining in and having a ball, too. Jill felt pleased at that thought, as Mum hadn't had much fun since Dad died three years ago.

She sipped her hot chocolate and gazed into the flames in the fireplace, imagining her mum's face once again wreathed in smiles. The thought cheered her, and she smiled to herself.

'Penny for them,' Andrew said.

'I was thinking of home.'

'Homesick?'

'No.' She shook her head. 'This is all too different and interesting to be homesick. Just... thinking about Mum, and wondering how she and Linda are getting on.'

Andrew saw the pensive look that crossed Jill's features and he reached his hand across the coffee table and placed it on hers. 'They'll be getting on like a forest fire,' he said.

She raised her eyes and looked at him. 'I expect so.'

She was aware of the warmth of his hand on hers, of the warmth of his being near to her, of the warmth of Andrew as a person. Was this really the man she thought of as Mr. Bossy? Of the man who was not pleased to have her work with him? Of the boss who made her work so hard, her head was spinning every night?

He was none of these things at the moment; he was simply Andrew, her neighbour and friend of Linda, who had taken her to the Tattoo and was now plying her with hot chocolate to chase the chill from her body. And that chill was disappearing fast.

She seemed to be melting as she looked into his dark brown eyes, and she felt her face flush with the glow from the fire and from the extraordinary leaps and somersaults her emotions were performing. Her normal Aussie *sang-froid* was evaporating along with the rain on her hair, and her brain cells were turning to mush.

Jill slipped her hand away from his and broke his gaze. She took another sip of her hot chocolate and cast her mind about for something to talk about.

'So, you feel it's quieter sleeping at the back of the building?' she asked brightly.

Andrew stared at her. 'Yeah,' he said, 'there's not so much early morning noise. Don't you get woken up by it?'

'Saves me having to set my alarm clock. I can tell what time it is by the sounds. Screech of van's brakes, seven thirty. They're delivering to the cafe opposite. Metal shutters being raised, eight o'clock. The newsagent's is opening. Smell of coffee, eight-fifteen. Early morning people buying a cup on their way to work. Commentary from the tour bus, it's after nine and I've slept in.'

Andrew laughed. 'I never thought of it like that. I suppose Linda does the same, though she never keeps nine-to-five hours. She writes when she feels like it. Sometimes, she's still in her dressing gown late in the afternoon. And her light is often on way into the night.'

'She won't like the hours we keep in Oz,' Jill said. 'Mum's up at dawn to feed the chooks and get work done before it gets too hot in summer. It will be all right at the moment, it's the end of winter and the temperature doesn't get much above twenty-five degrees.'

'We're lucky to get anything like that here in summer,' he said. 'Haven't you felt it cold since you've been here?'

She nodded. 'My feet and hands in particular.' She wriggled her toes in Linda's cosy slippers and held out her hands.

Immediately, Andrew took one again. 'It's warm now,' he said, as he rubbed the back of her hand. 'Positively hot, in fact.'

His hands felt hot to Jill, too, and an electric tingle shot up her arm. She tried to pull her hand away, but he was holding it firmly with one and stroking it with the other. Then he pulled her to her feet and moved round the coffee table to her side.

'Thanks for the drink,' she gabbled, as she found herself in all too close proximity to him. Funny, he seemed taller and bulkier the nearer to him she was; in fact, she felt overwhelmed by him. So much so that she found herself being pulled towards him by an invisible rope which wound round her and drew her tighter to him.

'I've dried off now,' she babbled, her mind completely liquid. 'And I'm warm, too.'

'You're hot,' Andrew whispered in her ear as he bent towards her. 'Absolutely boiling hot. So hot, you're burning me up.'

His lips came nearer, and Jill closed her eyes and gave in to the compelling urge to feel his mouth on hers. Her face lifted towards his and waited for the explosion she expected from the touch of their lips. Nothing happened. After a few seconds, she opened her eyes to find him staring into them, a perplexed look on his face.

'Why are we doing this?' he asked. 'Do you like me, or are you just playing with me?'

Jill didn't know what to say. Did she like him, or didn't she? A moment ago, she had given herself up to him longing for his kiss, yet before that, she would never have believed such a situation could happen.

'Well?' He was still extremely close to her, so close she could feel his breath.

'Yes and no,' was her answer. 'Sometimes I like you, and sometimes I don't. I never know what to expect from you. One minute you're friendly and funny and good company, the next you're rude and withdrawn and dismissive. What am I expected to think of you when you're as changeable as the Scottish weather? I don't know what you're up to, but it's not very attractive. In fact, it's very off-putting. Is there something wrong with you?'

His arms left her waist where they had been encircled,

and he shrugged. 'Typical Aussie bluntness,' he said. 'Well, at least I know where I stand.' He picked up his cup and drained it. 'You'd better go now in case I try anything else and you're in an I-hate-Andrew mood.'

'Now you're the childish one,' Jill replied. 'My feelings about you are all mixed up. No, I didn't like you at first, especially after you were so rude about your parking space, but I've got over that and now I find I'm beginning to change my mind at times like now. But then you change back to the old stuffed shirt Andrew. I haven't come over here to have my feelings mucked about by you. I don't need all that crap. If you've an explanation about why you blow hot and cold all the time, at least be upfront about it and explain. But don't expect me to be a mind-reader.'

Jill walked out of the room, slammed the front door behind her, and crossed the landing to her own flat. She was shaking so much she could scarcely get the key in the lock. She ratcheted away at it, praying that Andrew wouldn't follow her before she got inside.

When at last she managed to open the door, she ran into the bedroom and flung herself on the bed.

What happened there? One minute they were all friendly, chatting away; the next, she was falling into his arms and swooning to be kissed; and then suddenly, she was berating his character to his face and stomping out of the door and away. She was even more confused than before.

10

Andrew was wretched. He leant his back against his door and covered his face in his hands. What was he thinking of? She was a temptress, lulling him into thinking they could be friends, that she liked him, that she wanted him to kiss her... But he'd stopped himself just in time, and he'd got her to admit she didn't like him – sometimes, at any rate.

She'd spoken the truth about him. He did blow hot and cold, and it was all because of Nicola and his feelings. He'd been so upset when they broke up, even though he had been the one to do it. She had been the one in the wrong. He didn't know if he could bear the emotional turmoil of another relationship.

Damn and blast the typical male Scottish reserve. He'd been brought up to keep a stiff upper lip and not let his emotions all hang out, but when it mattered, he couldn't be honest about his feelings. Jill had only spoken the truth; she'd been honest with him. And if he wanted any kind of relationship with her, he was going to have to open up about it all and not bury himself in his work, which was his usual default mode when faced with such a situation.

He went into the lounge and picked up her cup. It was still half full of hot chocolate, though lukewarm would be the better description. She hadn't even finished it before she'd stormed out the door.

He cupped his hands round the drink, aware that her lips had touched its side, her hands had held it just as he was, and he wanted to smash it against the white walls. Andrew stopped himself with a wry smile. It wouldn't do to have a chocolate stain constantly reminding himself of this evening. He had enough memories without that.

The doorbell peeled into the silence. Andrew glanced at his watch. Who could be at his door at this time of night? He hadn't heard footsteps coming up the stairs nor had the outside buzzer sounded. It could only be…

Jill stood on the doormat, an embarrassed smile hovering over her features.

'I'm sorry,' she said to him. 'I know I'm blunt and I speak my mind without thinking, but I didn't mean what I said. Well, I suppose I did, but…' she faltered. 'I can't get this right. You were kind enough to take me to the Tattoo and then invite me in for a drink, and I managed to upset you by being rude, and I'm very sorry. I apologise.' She ground to a halt, the last of her breath exhaling like a sigh.

There was a silence that seemed to go on forever. Then Andrew spoke, a nerve twitching in his jaw as he did so. 'Thank you for that. I accept your apology. Now we can both sleep easy in our beds. I'll see you in the office tomorrow. Goodnight.' And shut the door.

FOR THE SECOND time in a few minutes, Jill had been shut

out of his flat. She stomped back into hers and slammed the door.

'What an up-yours prig of a man!' she shouted at the television. 'What a stuffy, self-centred pain in the butt of an excuse for a man!' Then she picked up a cushion and punched it around the room, before collapsing on the couch and bursting into tears.

11

T hings were cool between them for the next few days. Jill did what he asked of her in the office, said as little as possible to him, and made sure she didn't leave at the same time as him. But her mind wasn't fully on her work. Why was she so disturbed by his response to her apology? Had she really hoped that it would be enough? That he would once more take her in his arms and bend his mouth to hers? Why did she care so much? What was he to her, apart from her boss? And a friend of Linda's. And her nearest neighbour. Too much. Far too much. There needed to be distance between them. A great deal of distance. Like from Edinburgh to Sydney.

Her organisation of the Fringe party was half-hearted. She couldn't find any enthusiasm for the night which was looming ever closer. She had caterers arranged and a plentiful supply of wines and beer, and the invites were all out; there had already been a great many acceptances.

Obviously, Andrew's parties were something to be anticipated for a variety of reasons. People like Sam O'Connor were keen to come and meet up with the agents and producers who would be there, and others came, knowing that the company and the *craic* were good, and the food and drink plentiful.

The morning of the party, a Saturday, she allowed herself a short lie-in before breakfasting and heading over to the venue to check the arrangements. After all, it would be a late night and Jill wanted to be fresh enough to enjoy it – or, at least, make sure that everything ran smoothly. Most of all, she wanted Andrew to have no cause for complaint about her arrangements. Though, the way she was feeling, she wouldn't have cared if he sacked her on the spot.

Yet that still left the fact of his proximity outside working hours. She would need to move flats if she really wanted to get away from him, but that would be far too expensive. She had checked out the cost of renting in the city and been appalled at the prices for even a tiny apartment. So, she reasoned that if she stuck with the job for a few weeks more, she would have saved enough for a short trip around some of the Scottish landmarks she was so keen to see.

The venue was a pub in the Old Town, not too far from the Canongate. Jill enjoyed the walk in the fresh morning air, and her spirits began to lift as she crossed the Royal Mile and headed down the steps to the hostelry. On entering, she was surprised to see party balloons saying Happy Birthday and 21 Today being blown up by a couple of the bar staff.

'Hello,' she said to a young blonde girl, wearing jeans and a t-shirt which said Birthday Boy on it. 'Are these the balloons for the Fringe party tonight?'

'For the what party?' the girl replied. 'They're for the owner's son's 21st tonight. It's a surprise party for him.'

'Here?' Jill asked.

The girl nodded as she blew up another blue balloon.

Jill's heart raced. Surely not? Surely there must be a mix-up. Surely it couldn't be her mistake. 'Is the manager in?' she asked.

The other girl pointed to a door at the back of the pub. She continued to blow up balloons, her face reddening with the effort.

Jill pushed her way through a sea of colourful, bubbling balloons to the door, and knocked.

'Come in,' said a woman's voice.

'I'm Jill Kennedy,' she said. 'PA to Andrew MacCallum-Blair. I'm here to check on arrangements for the Fringe party he's giving.'

The manager opened her diary. 'Next Saturday,' she said. 'The 6th. Yes, I've got it marked down here.'

Jill's heart sank. 'The 6th,' she groaned. 'Is that what I booked? Not tonight?'

'Definitely not tonight. It's the owner's son's 21st, and we were told to keep tonight free for it. There's no way I'd have booked you in for tonight.'

'You haven't got a spare room anywhere that we could use?'

The other woman shook her head. 'Anyway, all the staff are either serving at it, or here as guests. In fact, we're totally closed to the public tonight.'

'What on earth am I going to do?' Jill wailed. 'I've got over 50 guests turning up tonight at 8 o'clock and nowhere for them to go.'

'Sorry,' said the manager. 'But we can't have you here. And I take it you'll want to cancel the booking for next week?'

Jill nodded. 'Thanks anyway,' she said, as she turned to go.

'I hope you find somewhere else,' the manager said to Jill's retreating back. 'Good luck.'

She headed straight back home, settled herself with her laptop, and started searching for Edinburgh venues. Unfortunately, many of them were already fully booked, or were too small, or too far out, or just not suitable. Just as she was running out of ideas, an email dropped into her mail box.

Automatically, she clicked on it. Linda. More news of her goings-on in Australia, and a story about a party she and Jill's mum, Patricia, had laid on for friends and neighbours. Jill marvelled at Linda's ability to persuade her mum to do such a thing. Linda went on;

I hope you'll have a party at the flat some time. Andrew and I often combine our resources, as it were, and throw a party across the landing. We always invite all the neighbours as it can get quite noisy. But they're a great crowd, as you probably realise, and love meeting all Andrew's interesting cronies.

A light bulb flashed in Jill's head.

'Bless you, Linda,' she said. 'That's a great idea.'

Fortunately, she'd brought her memory stick home with her from the office, so it was a matter of only a few moments before emails and phone calls were redirecting caterers and guests to the new venue. There was only one small matter left to deal with. Telling Andrew.

She delayed it for as long as possible. First, she set off down to Princes Street, where she'd spotted a party shop on one of her earlier explorations of the shopping area. She stocked up on balloons, streamers, strings of lights, and a huge banner that said Party Time in gold letters. Tied across the banisters, it would guide the guests to their landing.

Laden, she tiptoed up the stairs, hoping that Andrew would not take it upon himself to go out just then and come face-to-face with her and her spoils. She wasn't quite ready to face him yet.

Then, up and down the stairs she went, tapping at each of the neighbours' doors. As Linda had said, they were a cheery crowd, and delighted that her niece was carrying on what seemed to be quite a tradition of party-throwing.

'I'd better get my voice in tune,' said the lady in one of the top flats. 'Linda always liked when I sang some of the old Scots ballads.'

'That will be great,' Jill said. 'And Sam O'Connor will be there, so he can sing some Irish songs.'

'Oh, I'm not up to his standard,' the lady, whose name was Iris, said. 'I just sing at parties.' She put her hand on Jill's arm. 'And usually only when I've had a few drams!' Her laughter followed Jill back down the stairs.

Now there was only Andrew left. What should she tell him? That she'd messed up on the venues? That there had been a double booking – which wasn't strictly true, but left her with less egg on her face than otherwise? That she'd had this marvellous idea to make it just like one of Linda's parties – very informal and loads of fun?

She was still swithering about what to say as she rang his doorbell. She waited. Nothing. She rang again, willing him to answer the door. Still nothing. He was out. Definitely out.

'Well, I hope he comes back before the guests start arriving, or he's in for a shock,' she muttered to herself as she crossed the landing to her flat. But what if he goes straight on to the pub, thinking that that's where it's being held? What if he ends up in the middle of a 21st birthday party?

For the rest of the day, she busied herself moving anything valuable of Linda's out of the way, clearing surfaces so that the caterers could set out the food and drink, and attempting to blow up balloons until she had no puff left. She strung lights round the balustrade on the landing, giving a cheerier glow to the area.

She was just tying the big banner to the banisters outside their flats, when she heard the outer door open and footsteps heading towards the stairs. This had to be Andrew.

Peering over, she could see the top of his head as he climbed the stairs. He disappeared momentarily beneath her as he crossed the first landing to the next flight. Her heart was pounding so much she wouldn't have been surprised if he heard it. Then he began the ascent to their landing.

Halfway up, he seemed to sense her presence, because he stopped and looked up. His gaze took in the merry little lights glinting around the brass balustrade, the gold of the banner on the banisters, and Jill standing there like a frightened kangaroo in a car's headlights, mesmerised by the oncoming danger.

'What the—!' Andrew's eyes swept round the scene again as if he couldn't take in what he was seeing. Then he climbed the rest of the stairs and stood in front of her.

'Am I to assume from what I'm seeing that the party's here?'

Jill forced herself to smile. 'Yes,' she said in as bright a voice as she could manage, given that her throat wanted to close up completely, 'didn't I tell you?'

'You've cocked it up,' he said. 'You've made an absolute dog's dinner of the arrangements, haven't you?'

Jill hung her head. 'Yes,' she said in almost a whisper. God, she hated confessing her mistake to him. 'I made a mistake on dates, and there's a 21st party on at the venue tonight so they just can't fit us in. I've tried everywhere else. I've spent ages phoning round, but there's nowhere else.'

She knew she was gabbling but she couldn't stop. 'So then, Linda emailed and said she hoped we'd have a party like you used to with her, and I've emailed and phoned round everybody and they're all coming here at eight...' she tailed off at last.

Andrew looked at his watch. 'Right, that doesn't give us much time,' he barked. 'Let's get moving. I'll talk to you about this shambles in the office on Monday. Meantime, we've work to do.'

And work they did. Andrew set Jill to cleaning bathrooms and kitchens, while he moved furniture and set out as many chairs as he could borrow from the neighbours. They all seemed to be quite used to shifting TVs and coffee tables out of the way into the other flats, while a procession of chairs and side tables made their way into Jill and Andrew's.

Iris brought down a karaoke machine with numerous CDs and a couple of mics – 'You never know, maybe Sam O'Connor and I can sing a duet!' – and set it up in Andrew's lounge.

The caterers arrived in plenty of time, and by the time the first guest arrived, the whole area had been transformed into a welcoming and unusual venue. Jill had changed into black trousers and a sparkly gold top from Linda's wardrobe, set off with killer gold heels (Linda's again), and a pair of dangly earrings.

Andrew, she noticed, gave her a brief admiring glance as he carried a tray of glasses into the kitchen, while she couldn't help but admire his slim but firmly muscled body in dark jeans and a plain white t-shirt. Casual but perfect, she thought. Pity she was completely in his bad books.

Before long, music was carrying across the landing, and streams of guests were climbing the stairs. Groups of people gathered in Jill's kitchen or out on the landing, holding drinks and chatting. In Andrew's lounge, Iris was dancing with some young guys that Jill recognised as being from a rather satirical revue that had both shocked and delighted the critics.

Jill herself had chatted to girls from an American modern dance troupe, several businessmen who were interested in funding new talent, and a retired gentleman who had come to see his old neighbour on the ground floor and been inveigled into joining the party. An eclectic mix if ever there was one, Jill thought, as she surveyed the buzzing and satisfying scene.

People wandered between flats, or collected around someone holding court with some good stories of the Festival. Sam O'Connor didn't need much persuading to tune his guitar and strum a few chords, before launching into some of his repertoire. Soon everyone was joining in the choruses – some loudly, some totally out of tune, and others providing harmonies which echoed around the close. It didn't matter whether you could sing or not, the point was to enjoy yourself.

Other guests stepped forward to perform, too. Andrew sang a bawdy Scots song, not a word of which Jill could understand, which was probably just as well given the gales of laughter that accompanied each verse. He looked very relaxed and thoroughly enjoying himself, quite different to the Andrew of earlier and to the Mr. Bossy Jill had first set eyes on.

Iris informed Jill that it was an old Scottish tradition to do a party piece, and asked her what she could sing. Jill was startled. She hadn't sung anything since her school concert, when she was eight and played a singing mouse.

'I don't think I…' she began.

'Nonsense!' said Iris. She clapped her hands loudly and

yelled to the throng, 'Time for an Aussie song now. Let's hear it for our hostess, Jill!'

Everybody cheered and, before she knew it, she was handed a mic and silence descended. They were waiting for her to sing. Andrew was watching her, a glass in his hand and a wry smile on his face. What on earth could she possibly sing? She cleared her throat, held the mic close to her mouth, and sang just about the only song she thought they'd all know. She was right.

ONCE A JOLLY SWAGMAN camped by a billabong,
Under the shade of a coolibah tree,
And he sang as he sat and waited by the billabong,
Who'll come a-waltzing Matilda with me?

THE CHORUS RAISED THE ROOF. She was sure Linda could hear it in Australia. When she finished, the applause was loud and hearty, and she was delighted when Andrew raised his glass to her. Had she totally redeemed herself in his eyes? She felt even better when, as the wee small hours of the morning crept in and people started heading home, the comments were positive and very complimentary.

'Best party ever.'

'You take after your aunt, dear. This was as good as any of hers.'

Sam O'Connor gave her a bear hug and whispered, 'Thanks for asking me. I think I've got a recording contract out of this, plus several bookings in London and Birmingham.' Jill was delighted for him.

Iris was in seventh heaven. She'd sung several songs along with Sam, and he'd given her a copy of his latest CD and promised to keep in touch. 'What a lovely young man he is,' she confided in Jill. 'Almost as nice as Andrew, though he takes some beating. Lucky the lady who catches him.' And she winked at Jill as she started to climb the stairs to her flat.

Then it was only Jill and Andrew left. The strings of lights were still twinkling, there were still a few balloons hanging forlornly from where she'd tied them, the gold party banner had acquired a few rips and several unidentified stains, and the remains of the food and drink were spread everywhere across the two flats. Jill began to gather up some glasses and plates, but Andrew stopped her.

'Let's just leave it till the morning. I want to talk to you.'

'What, now?' He wasn't going to start telling her off now surely?

She followed him into his lounge. It wasn't so neat and tidy and minimalist now, with several glasses stained with dregs on the mantelpiece, plates with chicken bones and olive stones on the floor, the coffee table, and even on the window ledges. It looked as if a good time had been had by one and all.

Andrew turned to her and took hold of her hands.

'I want to thank you for arranging an absolutely fabulous party and to apologise for my bad-temper, my bad behaviour, and anything else bad about me that you don't like.'

Jill stared at him, open-mouthed. He was apologising to her? Mr. Bossy Big-boots was actually saying sorry?

He must have seen her shock. 'I really do mean it. It was one of the best parties we've ever had, and there were some interesting and hopefully lucrative contacts made. Some people will owe you a great vote of thanks.'

Jill nodded, still shocked. 'Sam,' she said. 'He said he might get a contract from tonight.'

'Exactly. And it's all thanks to you.'

'Not entirely. You made up the guest list, I just did what you asked. Well, after a fashion,' she added, remembering the fiasco about the venue.

'But the party wouldn't have been so relaxed, and people wouldn't have mixed so well if we'd had it where you booked it originally.'

'Then, thank your neighbours. They really got things going.'

Andrew smiled at her. 'You're determined not to take any credit for it, are you? But I'm thanking you… like this.'

He pulled her towards him and bent his mouth to hers. Jill closed her eyes as his lips met hers. They were warm and sweet tasting, soft and tender, and kissed just the way she liked being kissed. She sighed gently and let herself draw even closer into his arms. Their kiss deepened, their mouths opened to each other, their bodies fitted themselves into each other, adjusting till closeness and warmth were satisfied. Heaven could not be any more perfect.

Their lips parted, their eyes opened, and they looked at each other in a new way; a new recognition taking over from the old. Mr. Bossy was gone, Mr. MacCallum-Blair was gone, only Andrew was left. Her Andrew. Jill smiled up at him and moved to kiss him again.

A loud buzz sounded.

Andrew drew apart from her. 'Who can be wanting in at this time of the night?' he said. He walked into the hall, flipped the switch on the entry phone, and said sharply, 'Yes?' into the speaker.

'Police,' came the tinny reply.

12

Two sets of heavy police boots made their way up the stairs. Jill could hear the footsteps coming closer and her heart contracted. What bad news could they be bringing? Andrew was out on the landing, impatiently waiting their ascent.

'Had a bit of a party, sir?' the young man asked. 'Looks like it's been a good one.'

Without answering, Andrew led them into the lounge where Jill was sitting on one of the leather couches.

'What's the problem?' he asked, gesturing them towards the other couch where they made themselves comfortable.

'Nothing to worry about, sir,' said the older woman constable, taking charge. 'The office downstairs from yours was the subject of an attempted break-in this evening. They weren't successful, and your offices weren't touched at all.' She took out her notebook and checked what was written there. 'They attempted to gain entry at the back by smashing the window of a basement store-room. Do you or your staff have access to that store?'

Andrew shook his head. 'As far as I know, it's not used even by the company on the ground floor.'

'Apex Insurances?'

'Yes,' he replied. 'They've been there longer than me. Haven't you checked with them?'

'The CID are with the owners as we speak.' Her tone implied what she thought of that branch, but her expression was inscrutable.

'Did you or your staff notice anything suspicious at any time?'

Andrew shook his head. 'I wasn't there at all today. Were you, Jill?'

'No.'

The policewoman focused her attention on Jill. 'You work there, too?'

'She's my PA,' Andrew broke in.

'Temporary, acting,' Jill added.

'How long have you worked with Mr. MacCallum-Blair?'

'Only a few weeks.'

'Where were you before?'

'Australia.'

'Look here,' Andrew remonstrated. 'Jill came highly recommended from the Elite Employment Agency, which I always use for my temps. There's no way she's got anything to do with tonight's incident.'

'We have to check everything, sir,' said the policewoman with a knowing look.

She asked Jill for her full name, age and address, then snapped shut her notebook and stood up. The young constable reluctantly followed. He looked none too keen to head back out into the night.

'Thank you, sir, for your help and your time,' she said, leading the way to the door. 'I hope your party went well.'

'Very well,' said Andrew. 'Just the clearing up to do now.'

'Leave it till the morning,' said the young constable with a nod at Jill. 'Better get off to bed and get some shut-eye.'

'That'll do, Jimmy,' said the policewoman. 'Mr. MacCallum-Blair doesn't need any advice from whipper-snappers like you.'

Jill listened to the clump of feet down the stairs and sighed. The atmosphere had changed. No longer was it amorous and romantic, no longer loving and passionate with the hint of more to come.

Andrew shut the door and returned to the lounge. He squashed his hands into his pockets. 'I just hope I switched on the alarm system when I left. Maybe I should take a run over and check. If it's gone off, it will need resetting. Won't be long.'

With that, he grabbed his car keys and was gone.

'Well, I suppose I could start some of the clearing up,' Jill said to the empty room as she heard the sound of his car revving out the parking lot in the quiet of the night and turning into the Canongate. But after picking up some glasses and plates and trying to find space for them in the kitchen, she gave up, made herself a cup of tea, and curled up on the couch.

When Andrew returned half an hour later, Jill was stretched out, sound asleep, her cup untouched on the coffee table beside her.

He fetched the tartan rug they had covered their knees with at the Tattoo, and laid it over the sleeping figure. Then he bent down and kissed her brow.

'Sleep well, my darling,' he murmured. 'Sleep well.'

13

For a moment, Jill couldn't work out where she was when she woke. The sun was streaming through the curtains as usual, but they weren't the same curtains, nor was she in her bed. She felt the rough warmth of the tartan rug in her fingers as she looked around, and realised she was still in Andrew's flat.

Had he covered her with the rug? Her cold cup of tea stared at her, as did several party balloons dangling half-heartedly from where she'd fastened them on the wall. She sat up and stretched, her gold top incongruous in the light of a sleepy Sunday morning. She slipped her unwilling feet into Aunt Linda's gold stilettos and hobbled into the hall then paused, unsure whether to tiptoe out or to look in on Andrew and tell him she was leaving.

Jill was still undecided when the bedroom door opened, and a sleep-tousled, unshaven Andrew emerged, yawning and stretching.

'Good morning,' she said. 'I hope you slept well.'

'Morning.' He ran his hand through his hair, leaving it

sticking up even more and headed off into the kitchen. Jill heard him running water into the kettle.

She called out, 'I'm going back to my flat. I'll come through later and give you a hand with the tidying up.'

'Ok,' came the reply.

Jill paused for a moment, wondering if he would come to the door with her, but he didn't emerge. She opened his door and stepped out on to the landing. It looked sad and bare now that everyone had gone, the strings of lights still wound round the balustrade, and the banner, limp and tattered, had slumped sideways like a drunk man. She was struggling to untie it from the banisters when she heard someone coming down the stairs from the upper flats. A pair of legs in green trousers emerged and Jill recognised Iris.

'Morning!' she called cheerily as she reached Jill's landing. 'I'm just off to get the Sunday papers and to clear my head. It was a great night, wasn't it?'

She looked at Jill, still wearing her party gear. 'You didn't get to bed then?' she asked, her eyebrows hitting her hairline.

'What? Oh yes, I had a few hours' sleep. I just couldn't be bothered changing into my pyjamas. It didn't seem worth it.' No way was she going to admit to sleeping on Andrew's couch. Iris nodded and carried on down the stairs. As soon as Jill heard the outside door slam behind her, she let herself into her flat.

It was as messy as Andrew's. Dirty glasses decorated every surface, empty wine and beer bottles were stashed in the kitchen beside the bin, plates of half-eaten food were piled on the work surfaces, paper napkins and beer tops and burst balloons were strewn throughout every room.

Jill had a quick shower, first removing three red balloons that had somehow ended up tied to the shower head. Then on with her jeans and top, and out with the black bin bags.

By the time she had returned Linda's flat to a semblance of normality and been relieved to see that there was no long-term damage to anything, she was starving. She threw on her jacket and headed out to the coffee shop across the street. Returning with two cups of coffee and four bacon rolls, she knocked on Andrew's door.

'Breakfast,' she said when he opened it. He, too, was dressed in old jeans and top, and was obviously still in the middle of the clearing up.

'Jill,' he grinned, 'you are a life-saver.'

They sat on stools at the breakfast bar, and never had bacon rolls tasted so good. Soon, there was nothing left, and she and Andrew sipped their coffees feeling full and contented.

'I've finished clearing up in my flat,' Jill told him. 'I can give you a hand in here.'

'There's not much left to do. The caterers should be here soon to pick up the plates and glasses, and when they've gone the place will look much better. We can take the garbage down to the bins, return the chairs and side tables to the neighbours, and then the day's our own. What would you like to do?'

Jill hid her surprise at Andrew's eagerness to spend time with her, but remembered all too clearly the kisses they had shared last night and felt a tingle deep inside her.

'There's so much to see. I'd like to visit Holyrood Palace and see where David Rizzio was murdered in front of Mary Queen of Scots.'

'That's just a few yards away from here,' said Andrew. 'There's also the new Scottish Parliament just opposite it, but let's keep that for a rainy day. It's too nice to be inside. What do you say to a walk up Arthur's Seat?'

'Sounds good!' Jill had noticed the great hill that rose just beyond the Canongate, and which looked rugged and wild and untamed. She'd seen people walking up the numerous paths that flanked its sides. 'Can we go right to the top?'

'If you're fit,' replied Andrew.

'You're asking an Aussie girl if she's fit?' was Jill's reply. 'Just watch me. I'll leave you for dead.'

Fit though she claimed to be, Jill was nevertheless grateful for Andrew's hand as they climbed up the steeper than expected slope to the top. It was hard to believe that the city was just below them. They walked through rough grass and stunted shrubs, with here and there outcrops of the tough weather-worn rock that formed the hill.

'Why is it called Arthur's Seat?' Jill asked when they paused to admire the view and to catch their breath.

'Allegedly it's after King Arthur,' Andrew replied, sitting down on a flat piece of rock. 'But no-one can be sure. It's a volcano, by the way,' he added, as Jill was about to join him on the rock.

'What?' she said, as she quickly straightened up.

'It's ok,' Andrew laughed. 'Been extinct for centuries. No chance of it rumbling back into life.'

Still, Jill took a bit more care as she followed him up to the top.

Reaching there, a cooling breeze fanned them and kept the clouds moving. The panorama stretched to the Firth of Forth and beyond to the coast of Fife. Beyond the skyline of the city, the sea glinted and sparkled in the glimpses of sun which came and went in the white puff of clouds.

'See that island in the middle of the Forth?' Andrew pointed to a roundish lump of rock. Jill nodded. 'That's the Bass Rock. It's famous for its gannet colony. About 150,000 of them nest there every year.'

Turning away from the sea, they could have been in the middle of nowhere. Bleak moorland stretched as far as they could see, with hills rising in the distance. It was hard to believe that a city was so close.

'I guess the Highlands must look like this,' Jill said.

'Yes and no. Haven't you seen them? Then you're in for a surprise. They're the same and as different as you can imagine. It all depends on where you are and what the weather's like.'

'When I've earned enough money from the job, I'm going to take off in Linda's car and travel right round the country. I've heard there are plenty of hostels and cheap bed and breakfasts I can stay in.'

Andrew smiled at her. 'Sounds idyllic. Reminds me of my student days, when we used to drive up to the Cairngorms to go climbing. We stayed in bothies – basic mountain huts – and cooked over a fire or on camping stoves. The food always tasted tremendous.'

'Why don't you come with me?' Jill said.

He shook his head. 'No can do. I can't leave the business for that length of time, not when I'm still building it up. Anyway, I'm having a break in a couple of weeks' time, once I tie up all the loose ends around the Festival. Margery is giving me a loan of her cottage in the Trossachs so that I can get away from it all.'

'What are the... what did you call it?'

'Trossachs. It's a beautiful area not far north of Glasgow, with lochs and mountains. Loch Lomond is part of it. It's handy for those of us who live in cities, and yet quiet and picturesque and wild. I'm looking forward to going.'

Jill mentally filed it away as another must-see place. Goodness, she was going to have to carry on working for quite a while if she was going to be able to afford to visit everywhere she wanted.

It was a lovely day. Jill enjoyed Andrew's company and, as Linda had said, he was very knowledgeable about his country and city. They ambled down the hill, back to the city, and made their way back to the Canongate, passing the Palace of Holyrood on the way.

'The Queen stays there every summer for a short while,' Andrew told her. 'There are always some garden parties and official ceremonies.'

'Is it still in use?' Jill stared through the grand iron railings at the imposing gothic-style palace.

'Of course. The public don't see the private apartments, but you can visit the public ones where the dinners and investitures are held.'

Five minutes later, they were climbing the stairs to their flats.

'How about dinner tonight?' Andrew asked. 'I don't know about you, but all that climbing has worked up an appetite.'

'Me, too,' Jill agreed.

'I know a nice little place not far from here that serves wonderful French-style food. Do you fancy that?'

'Yes,' Jill said eagerly. 'I haven't tried that. What's it like?'

'Delicious. I'll make a booking for seven, shall I? That will give us time to shower and change, and even catch up on a bit of sleep after last night.'

'I'll see you then,' Jill said, as she unlocked her door. She waltzed into her bedroom and tumbled onto the bed. What a great day out this has been, she thought. How could I ever think Andrew was a Mr. Bossy-boots?

She stretched out on the bed and replayed the climb up Arthur's Seat, trying hard to remember all that Andrew had told her. She must email her mum and tell her all about what she'd seen.

14

A buzzing rang in her head. She thought it must be a bee, but it wouldn't go away. She tried to wave her arms at it, but they were heavy and the noise kept on. Jill opened her eyes and realised it was someone at the door. She pulled herself off the bed and staggered sleepily towards the noise. When she finally managed to open the door, Andrew was waiting there, fresh-shaven and changed, ready for dinner.

His jaw dropped when he saw her.

'Don't tell me you're just awake,' he said. 'Our table's for seven. How could you sleep so long?'

Jill was instantly fully awake. 'No!' she said. 'I didn't mean to... How long have I got?'

'Two minutes. Hurry up.' Andrew strode into the lounge and sat down, his face revealing his annoyance. Jill flew into the bedroom and hauled off her clothes. Throwing on a short skirt and summery silk blouse, she dashed lip gloss on her mouth, sprayed perfume liberally over herself, and ran a brush through her hair.

She took a deep breath and sauntered as leisurely as she could into the lounge.

'Ready,' she said with a smile.

Andrew looked up surprised, glanced at his watch, and rose. 'Two minutes exactly,' he said as they left the flat and headed down the stairs. 'I'm impressed.'

'I don't go for the fashion-plate look,' she said with a grin. '*Au naturale* is more my style.'

The fresh air blew the rest of her cobwebs away. She still felt a bit other-worldly after her sudden awakening and mad dash to get ready, but the short walk to the restaurant revived her.

La Vie Francaise was situated in a basement, entered by some steep narrow steps. The maître d' met them at the door and ushered them to a table for two in a discreet little corner of the restaurant, and settled them there. He handed them a menu each and signalled for the drinks waiter.

'I would never have known this place was here,' Jill said as she looked around. It was simply decorated, with scenes of Paris on the walls and plain white linen table-cloths, a candle and a spray of summer flowers on the table.

'It's got a great reputation,' Andrew said. 'It doesn't need to do much in the way of advertising or décor, as the food is so good. French country cooking at its best. Let's order. I'm really hungry. Those bacon rolls were a long time ago.'

The evening passed very pleasantly in a haze of red wine, delicious hearty casseroles, and to finish, spun-sugar desserts and rich dark chocolate. They wended their way home through the summer twilight, the streets still busy with people enjoying the long evening light.

Conversation had been easy. Jill told him about her

family and life in Australia, and even confessed to exaggerating her abilities in order to get the job with him.

'Though I didn't know it was you at the time,' she said, her tongue loosened by the wine. 'I thought you'd be some middle-aged, balding guy.'

'What a disappointment for you when you saw me then,' he said.

'Not as much as it was for you,' she retorted, remembering his 'Good God, not you!' when he had seen her.

Andrew paused in the street and turned her to look at him. 'I didn't mean it quite like that,' he attempted to explain. 'I just didn't think we could work together as well as live so close.' Not for anything was he going to disclose his real reasons. Later perhaps, when – if – things turned out okay.

They made the rest of the journey home in silence, each wrapped up in their own thoughts. Jill was unsure whether or not Andrew had been completely truthful in his explanation. Why couldn't he just say sorry for being rude and leave it at that? And why did he find 'sorry' such a hard word to say? Did he always have to be right about everything? She sneaked a glance at his profile as they walked along. There was that tic again in the muscle in his jaw, a sure sign that he was stressed. What did he have to be stressed about? They'd had a lovely day, a lovely meal, and now what had been a lovely evening was rapidly disappearing down the plughole.

Jill decided to attempt to salvage it before it coloured everything.

'Fancy a coffee?' she asked, as they made their way up the stairs. 'And I've put some pictures of Oz on the computer, if you'd like to see them.'

'No, no thanks. Another time.' He stared at a point somewhere above Jill's head. 'I think I'll have a reasonably early night. After all, tomorrow's Monday and it's quite a busy week ahead.'

He nodded at her and walked across the landing to his flat. The door slammed shut behind him before Jill had even got her key in her lock.

'Bloody heck,' she told the mirror on the wall. 'He's back. Mr. Bossy. Mr. Grumpy. Mr. Make-Sure-I-Don't-Enjoy-Myself-Too-Much. What is it with Scotsmen that they're so buttoned up?'

She went into the kitchen and switched on the kettle for coffee, thinking that if it had been Grigor Lutsenko or even Sam O'Connor she'd had a meal with, they'd now be sitting in her kitchen with a coffee and talking. Or − thinking of Grigor's beautiful body − not talking, as the case may be. Instead, here she was, sitting on her lonesome and fuming about one lousy Scot who hadn't a romantic gene in his body. Typical.

She stirred her coffee furiously, spilling some of it onto the worktop. She reached over to pick up a cloth to mop it up, caught the handle of the mug, and the whole thing tipped onto the floor and smashed, spraying coffee everywhere.

'That's your fault you… you big… bossy…ba—'

The doorbell rang. 'Now what?' Jill yelled, stepping over the puddle of coffee and bits of mug, and heading for the door. She flung it open to find Andrew standing there, looking abashed.

'I'm sorry,' he said. 'You must think me crass. I apologise. I would like that coffee after all.'

'Well, you can't!' she shouted at him, and slammed the door.

Still furious, she stomped back to the kitchen and finished clearing up the mess, tipping the remains of the mug in the bin. She'd buy another one for Linda to replace the one she'd broken. I hope it's not a sentimental piece, she thought, as she opened the cupboard and took out another mug. She was, by this time, more than ready for a coffee.

This time, she carried it carefully through to where the computer sat, and opened up her emails. One from a girlfriend who had started work with a company in Sydney; one from her mum, full of news from home about the neighbours and her cousins, and what the cat had got up to. Nothing from Linda. Just as well. Jill wouldn't know what to say about Andrew.

What a changeable man. One minute, full of fun and easy to talk to, the next behaving like the grumpy tortoise in a childhood book of Jill's who pulled in his head and refused to come out. She tried to remember how the story ended. Was it a lettuce leaf that had tempted it, or a ripe tomato? She doubted if either would work with Mr. Bossy.

ANDREW DIDN'T MOVE. Had she really yelled at him and slammed the door in his face? Why had she done that? Was she really so angry with him?

He went back into his own flat and slumped on the couch. His first instincts had been right, he told himself. Keep her at a distance. He wasn't ready for another relationship. It was too soon since... So why had he talked himself into apologising for not accepting her offer of coffee when she asked? He'd been right to refuse at first, so why had he changed his mind? Why couldn't he just enjoy her company without wanting to take it further when he knew he wasn't ready for that? Nor had he planned for it.

He wanted to concentrate solely on building up his business, on giving himself a secure foundation on which to build a new life, and then he would, maybe, think about finding another partner. A woman who wouldn't cheat on him, who would be there for him, who would share his life and his dreams. Jill had turned up too soon, so it was up to him to stick to his guns, to remember his game plan, to be strong and decisive, and not be swayed by sparkling eyes and a feisty nature that threatened to leave him helpless with desire. No more days out, no more intimate dinners, no more partying, no more being together on their own.

Damn! That meant he would have to find another partner for the Caledonian Ball. He had intended to ask Jill to accompany him, sure that she'd enjoy the Scottishness of it all, the men in Highland dress, the women with tartan sashes over their evening gowns, the old Scottish set dances, the fun of dancing reels and jigs which became wilder as the evening wore on. Now he would have to take someone else and spend the whole time wishing it was Jill he was dancing with, swinging her round and catching her as she fell into his arms.

He slumped further into the couch. Why couldn't they just be friends, happy to be with each other when the occasion demanded or when they had some free time? It was his fault, though. He was the problem. He was the one who couldn't keep it easy-going and carefree. Look at tonight. He was the one who'd spoiled it by withdrawing into himself when it looked likely that there was a chance things could hot up. No wonder she was mad at him. She would never be able to know what he was thinking if he kept changing his behaviour towards her. No wonder she had yelled at him and slammed the door in his face. It was all his fault.

15

Monday morning in the office, and Jill could feel the tension in the air even although Andrew kept the door to his office firmly shut. She hadn't set eyes on him since she arrived promptly at nine o'clock, and she didn't mind if he never came out. Dorothy seemed oblivious to it all, however, and chatted away to Jill about the weekend's events. Jill managed to listen with half an ear to her tales of new curtains that wouldn't hang straight, and next door's dog disappearing for a couple of hours until he eventually returned home wet through.

'Down at the river, probably,' Dorothy said. 'He had to be bathed and he doesn't like it much. I could hear him through the wall howling his head off.' Dorothy lived in a terrace of houses where each was joined to the next in a row, and where the sound-proofing, Jill gleaned, was not particularly good. Jill wondered how people could live like that; she was used to having their next door neighbour across the other side of a paddock.

'Jill!' Dorothy's voice interrupted her musings.

'Sorry,' she said. 'I was thinking of something else.'

'You were in a wee dwam,' Dorothy smiled. 'I could see it in your eyes. Far away you were. Probably back in Australia.'

'I was in a what?'

'Dwam. Good Scots word for when your mind's elsewhere. Here in body but not in spirit.'

'I'm really sorry, Dorothy. I was listening, but then I just seemed to drift away.'

'Doesn't matter. You didn't miss anything terribly important.' Dorothy shuffled through the papers on her desk and selected a few to file. She rose and walked over to the filing cabinet beside the door that led to Andrew's office.

'What's eating the boss this morning?' she said, in a stage-whisper. 'Hasn't so much as stuck his nose out of the door.'

Jill shrugged and turned back to the work in front of her. No way was she going to enter into a conversation about the weekend. To Dorothy's enquiries about the party, she had just said that everything had gone well and some useful contacts had been made. No mention about the mix-up over the venue or how she and Andrew had spent Sunday.

When the postman delivered the mail later that morning, Dorothy picked up a large letter with delight.

'I know what this will be,' she announced. 'The tickets for the Caledonian Ball.'

Jill looked puzzled.

'Andrew always gets tickets for Margery and me and our husbands, as well as for himself and his partner,' Dorothy explained. 'It's a wonderful evening. All the men wear their kilts and we dress up in evening gowns, the food's wonderful, and the dancing goes on till two in the morning.' She paused. 'Maybe he'll have got you tickets as well. You'd love it, seeing as how you're Australian. And I could teach you some of the easier dances. Have you got someone you could bring?'

Jill shook her head. 'Pass,' she said. 'Anyway, if he's got tickets for Margery, then he wouldn't have got me any. I'm only temporary, after all.'

'Och, Andrew wouldn't be so petty. After all the hard work you've done for him? No, I'm sure he would have made sure you weren't left out.' Dorothy turned over the envelope in her hands and felt its weight. 'There will be a ticket for you in here.' She flipped through the rest of the mail. 'But I'd better hand this into him.'

She rapped on his door and disappeared into Andrew's office. Jill sighed and tried to concentrate on her work. She wasn't going to mind if she didn't get to go to the ball. It wasn't all that important. As she said, she was only the temp in the office; Margery was the one who deserved to go. So why were her eyes pricking with tears? So why did she feel disappointed?

Come on, Cinderella, she told herself, taking out her handkerchief and blowing her nose. It doesn't matter in the slightest if you don't go to the ball.

'Yes, you do,' said a little inner voice. 'You care a great deal.'

Anyway, I haven't anything to wear that would be remotely suitable. I didn't have room in my suitcase for an evening gown, even if I did have one.

'But Linda's wardrobe has some nice ones that would fit you.'

I haven't been asked, and I haven't got a partner.

'Maybe Andrew will ask you,' The little voice in her head persisted.

No, he most definitely won't. Jill stood up and marched into the tiny office kitchen to switch on the kettle for coffee.

She couldn't be doing with all this inner turmoil. She needed something to take her mind off it, even if it was only washing a couple of cups out and checking if the milk was fresh. It wasn't.

'I'm just nipping out for some milk,' she said to Dorothy, who was just leaving Andrew's office. 'I won't be long.'

16

Andrew picked up the phone and dialled.

'Margery,' he said when she answered. 'How are you?'

'Oh Andrew,' she said. 'Wait a moment while I switch *Thomas the Tank Engine* on.' The phone clattered down, and somewhere in the distance Andrew could hear Marjory's voice talking to Donald as she fiddled with the video. Then there was a fumbling, and some heavy breathing came on the line.

'Hi Donald,' Andrew said, guessing that the youngster had picked up the phone. 'Are you going to watch a video?' More heavy breathing before Margery came on the line again.

'There you are, darling,' she said. In the background, the introductory music to *Thomas the Tank Engine* played. 'You sit and watch it.'

'For a moment I thought you were talking to me,' Andrew said.

'Chance would be a fine thing,' she scoffed. 'I'm old enough to be your mother, if not your granny.'

'I like the older, more mature woman.'

'Well, there's older, more mature, and there's long past it. Anyway, I don't think my husband would approve. Now, how can I help you?'

'Everything's fine,' he replied. 'I just wanted to let you know that the tickets for the Caledonian Ball have arrived. You will manage this year, won't you?'

'Lovely, sure I will, and I'm looking forward to seeing you all again and, of course, meeting Jill. She sounds so nice, and she seems to be doing a great job. Although,' she paused, 'I think my daughter's coming home soon. The hospital are pleased with her and hopefully she can stay at home till the baby's born. So that means I can be back at work once she's settled. Will Jill be able to find work elsewhere? It seems such a shame to lose her, as she's done a magnificent job filling in for me. Still, she'll enjoy the ball. It's always such a great night out.'

While Margery chattered on, Andrew's head sank into his hand and he grimaced. He had received the usual six tickets that he ordered every year: two for Margery and her husband; two for Dorothy and hers; and two for himself and whoever he decided to invite to accompany him. He'd ordered them months ago, before Margery had had to take leave to help her daughter out, before the agency had sent Jill to be her replacement, before he had become fixated with her. Because that was what had happened, he admitted to himself. He didn't know where or when it had all happened, but there it was. He was fascinated by her, attracted to her, drawn to her, his mind was preoccupied by her, he was consumed by her, possessed even. What on earth was he to do?

He shifted the phone to his other ear, the better to try to concentrate on what Margery was saying.

'…so then we left it at that.'

Andrew gave what he hoped was a non-committal grunt. 'But I'd better let you get on with your work,' she continued, 'instead of prattling on like this. Say hello to the girls for me, and tell them I'll see them at the ball. Bye!'

Andrew put the phone down and turned to stare out of the long picture windows with their view of the gardens. He had intended to ask Jill to be his partner at the ball, but after last night when she'd yelled at him and slammed the door, he wondered if he should. And if he did, would she agree to come? And what about your resolution, he reminded himself, of not taking the relationship any further, of cooling things off, of keeping her at a distance? This was not what he had planned, not what he really wanted, though that niggling wee voice in his head kept telling him not to waste the opportunity, to let his heart rule for once, to go for it and see what happened.

Andrew MacCallum-Blair, he said sternly to himself, you are in a right mess. Get your head sorted out and do the right thing. But what was the right thing? Office politics demanded that he invite Jill, otherwise Margery, or for that matter, Dorothy, would never forgive him. They liked her, they could see no reason for her being left out, and further-more, it would be the height of bad manners to do so. But could he cope with his feelings if he took her and danced with her, and held her close, and maybe even kissed her again?

He groaned. He wasn't ready for another relationship, was he? He had barely recovered from the last one. There was still a scab somewhere in his heart that would bleed again if it was opened up. He really needed to get away from it all for a while.

Then he remembered. He jumped up from his seat and

walked over to the window. Down below in the street, a sweeper was gathering up the first leaves that had fallen from the trees. Summer was almost over. The Festival had finished. Things were quietening down, and he was going to get away from it all – to Margery's cottage in the Trossachs.

The day after the ball, he was heading north in his car for a blissful week of hill-walking and maybe a bit of fishing. Apparently, there was a good pub just across the road from the cottage, and he could eat there after a day in the fresh air and enjoy the company of other like-minded walkers, as well as the locals. It didn't really matter what happened at the ball, because he wouldn't be there to follow it through afterwards. He could take her to the ball, head off for a week, and when he came back, Jill would have moved on – literally perhaps, as well as metaphorically. Margery's daughter could possibly be home by then, and Margery back at the office. Jill might have already vanished from his life, apart from occasionally seeing her going up and down the stairs at the flat.

He would ask if she'd like to come to the ball with him, but he'd wait till he was sure she was speaking to him again. Whose turn was it to apologise? He'd say sorry again if it helped, but he wondered if Jill would regret her behaviour. Would she be prepared to say sorry for yelling at him? Did it matter whether she did or not? How was she feeling this morning? Had she calmed down? Was she still angry with him? Was she sulking, or – as Dorothy would put it – in the huff with him? He'd better check out how the land lay. He strode over to the door and headed out into the office. Only Dorothy was there, obviously deep in thought.

'Where's Jill?' he demanded.

Dorothy turned to look at him. 'She went out to get some milk, but she hasn't come back yet. I hope nothing's happened. In the meantime, you'll have to have your coffee black.'

Andrew shook his head. 'No thanks.'

17

Jill pounded along the street, clutching the carton of milk. The corner shop was only a few hundred yards from the office, but when she came out after making her purchase, she couldn't bear to return. Instead of turning left, she turned right and headed towards Princes Street Gardens. She wanted some fresh air and open spaces, and although the gardens would not be the quiet oasis she was seeking, at least there were trees and green spaces and flowers, even if they were herded into forming the floral clock – that magnificent timepiece set on a slope and made from showy annuals which bloomed over the summer months.

She crossed the busy thoroughfare that was Princes Street, with the shops and department stores on one side, and the gardens and the Scott Monument on the other. Above them all loomed the castle, and Jill lowered her eyes and tried not to think about the evening she and Andrew had watched the Tattoo from its heights.

She strode into the gardens and weaved her way among the leisurely crowds who, even at ten thirty in the morning, were meandering along the paths, stopping to admire the flowers, or sitting on the benches with a newspaper and a cup of coffee from Starbucks. Jill slowed her pace as the paths became quieter, the further away from Princes Street she walked. There were now only one or two people around her, and she took a deep breath and flopped onto an empty bench beside a bed of salvias and petunias. Their riotous colours cheered her and reminded her of her mum's colourful garden, along the shady side of the house back home.

What would her mum make of her situation, if she told her? What would she say if Jill said that her feelings for her boss were all mixed up, and not what one should be feeling for their boss at all? What exactly were her feelings for Andrew? Did she like him or not? And what were his feelings for her? She couldn't fathom him at all. One minute, he seemed to be enjoying her company; the next, he was cool towards her and desperate to get away. One minute, they were getting on like a wild fire; the next, one or other of them was annoyed and angry and upset. And, in her case, shouting at him and slamming the door in his face.

She would have to apologise to him for that. After all, he had come to say sorry to her, and she had rejected him. And all because she'd spilled her coffee on the floor and broken one of Linda's mugs.

She wished she could start all over again. She wished he hadn't shouted at her to move her car the first time she'd set eyes on him; she wished she hadn't taken the job with him – not that she'd known it was him when the Misses MacDonald had sent her. She wished she'd been firmer and walked out of his office when he'd been so rude to her when she'd arrived; she wished she hadn't gone to the Tattoo with him; not climbed Arthur's Seat with him;

not had dinner with him; not kissed him. Especially, not kissed him.

'Whit's wrang, hen?' The broad Scottish accent broke into her thoughts. Sitting himself down beside her on the bench was an old, dishevelled man, clutching something in a paper bag. Jill realised that there were tears running down her cheeks. She hastily pulled out a tissue and wiped them away.

'Nothing,' she said. 'I'm fine, really.'

The old man raised the paper bag to his lips and drank. Jill reckoned there must be a bottle of something alcoholic in there that he was keeping well hidden; public drinking was frowned upon by the local police. He saw Jill watching him and proffered the bag to her.

'Would ye like a wee dram?' he said.

Jill shook her head. 'I should be at work,' she replied. 'I only nipped out to get some milk,' she showed him the carton 'and suddenly I didn't want to go back.'

The old man shook his head. 'That's what work does tae ye,' he opined. 'Me, ah gave it up years ago.'

'Oh, it's not the work,' Jill said. 'I actually quite enjoy it. It's my boss. I can't understand him. One minute he's friendly, the next, pretty frosty. It's very disconcerting.'

'Is he old?'

'About thirty.'

'Guid-looking?'

'Yes, I suppose he is.'

'Married?'

'No.'

'Rich?'

'Well, it's his own business, and it seems to be doing well.'

'So, what's stopping ye?'

'What do you mean?'

'Marry him, hen. He sounds like a guid catch.'

Jill was flabbergasted. 'The last thing he'd do is marry me. And,' she drew herself up, 'I wouldn't marry him if he was the last man in Scotland.' She stood up. 'I'd better get back. Bye.'

As she left, she couldn't help but overhear him say, 'Ma money's on it, hen.'

No way, she thought as she half-walked, half-jogged back to the office. No way would she ever consider marrying Andrew, not that he was planning to ask her anytime in the near future, she was sure. Never, never, never would she say yes to him. She couldn't imagine what being married to him would be like: bossy, overbearing, moody, inhibited, rude. The adjectives flowed through her mind. Then she passed a young couple snuggling into each other in a doorway to kiss, and a sharp memory of Andrew's kiss shot through her. If she was married to him, she would kiss him every day; all day, if she wanted. And more. And very much more. She felt herself grow hot, and it wasn't from rushing back to the office either.

Dorothy must be wondering where I've got to, she thought, as she speeded up her pace even more. I must have been ages. And I hope Andrew hasn't noticed it's way past his coffee break. But he had. Andrew was standing on the front steps looking up and down the street. When he saw her, he started walking towards her.

'Where have you been?' he asked, frowning. 'Dorothy said you'd been away for ages.'

'I was getting some fresh milk,' Jill said, holding up the carton. 'And then… and then I took the long way back. I needed some fresh air. I-I was getting a headache.'

Andrew's frown deepened. 'Are you feeling all right now? You don't want to go home, do you?'

Jill put on a smile as she answered, 'No, I'm fine,' in as

hearty a voice as she could muster. 'And I could do with a coffee now.'

She tried to make her way towards the front door, but Andrew grasped her arm. 'Wait,' he said. 'I've got something I want to ask you.'

Jill stood, still clutching the carton of milk, and waited. He seemed to be having trouble getting out what he wanted to say. She watched as he stared at a point behind her, then at his shoes, and then took a deep breath in and looked straight at her.

'What I wanted to ask you was if... er... was if you would consider... if you would... I mean, I'd like it very much if you'd...'

Jill's mind went into overdrive. Surely not! Surely that old drunk man couldn't be right! What on earth could she say? Surely he wasn't going to...

'...come to the Caledonian Ball with me.'

She was so relieved that all she could do was nod her head at him several times. She felt like a nodding donkey, but Andrew didn't seem to mind, as his face broke into a big smile and his frown vanished.

'Great!' he said. 'Thank goodness. I didn't know if you were going to bite my head off or not.'

'Oh, I'm sorry about last night,' she said. 'I'd just spilt my coffee on the floor and broken one of Linda's mugs, and I was mad at you, too, for not coming in for coffee, which was silly as we'd had a lovely day out and a fabulous meal and I didn't want it all to be spoilt, and—'

Andrew put a finger on her lips. 'Shh!' he said. 'Let me get a word in. I want to apologise, too. I'm sorry I went all quiet and moody, but I had things on my mind. I'm sorry it all went pear-shaped, too.'

'I wish we could start all over again,' Jill blurted. 'We

always seem to be on the wrong foot with each other, and I never know where I am with you.'

They began walking up the steps to the office. 'That's my fault,' he said. 'I don't know where I am with myself half the time. You see, I suppose I should have told you before, but I—'

'Yoo-hoo!' came a shout from above. Dorothy was hanging out one of the windows in Andrew's office. 'Phone call for you, Andrew. It's that London agent that wants Sam on his books. Can you take it?'

Andrew ran up the rest of the stairs and into the building, leaving Jill to follow behind, wondering what he'd been about to confess to her. Would it have helped her to learn it? Would she have understood him more? Would it have explained his on-off behaviour towards her? She'd never know. Dorothy's interruption had made sure of that.

Jill slowly climbed the stairs and headed up to the office. When she got there, Dorothy had the kettle boiling and cups laid out with coffee in them.

'I thought you'd got lost,' she said. 'And I've been dying for a cup for ages. Here, give me the milk and let's get it open. Andrew will be even thirstier after he's finished on the phone.'

Dorothy and Jill sat at their desks with the coffees, but Dorothy didn't seem all that keen to talk, Jill noticed. So, there was a silence till Andrew joined them and perched on Jill's desk.

'That's Sam on his way to stardom, by the looks of things,' he said. 'The agent has got some television work for him, which should give him maximum exposure.'

'He deserves it,' said Jill. 'He's really good. Everybody loved his singing at the party. And Iris will be thrilled, too.'

'Iris?' said Dorothy. 'Iris who lives up the stairs from you? What's she got to do with it?'

Jill bit her lip. She could have kicked herself for her big mouth again. Of course, Dorothy didn't know about the fiasco over the party venue. But Andrew saved the day and spared Jill's blushes.

'She was at the party and sang a couple of duets with him. She's got quite a soft spot for him. I think she'll be his number one fan,' he said. He took a sip of his coffee and changed the subject. 'Are you looking forward to the ball, Dorothy?'

Jill was surprised to see her redden. 'Andrew's asked me to go with him,' she said, and immediately Dorothy's face brightened. 'So, you'd better tell me all about it. What do I wear?'

Dorothy launched into a long description of what the women wore to the ball. It seemed she had memorised every outfit from last year, as well as what she and Margery had chosen. 'Though, of course, you'll wear something really up-to-date,' she pointed out, 'something more elegant and… and sexy.'

Andrew got up from his perch on Jill's desk. 'I'll leave you two to it. I've got work to do, and I can't say women's fashions are my main interest in life. As long as you come in something partyish, and with your hair brushed, you'll do.'

'Huh, so much for the hours we women spend getting ready, if that's all the attention we get,' huffed Dorothy. 'I could come in my slippers and my apron, and you men wouldn't even notice.'

'It's not the clothes, it's the person inside them that counts,' Andrew said as he disappeared into his office with a mischievous grin on his face.

'Well, at least he's in a much better mood now,' Dorothy said. 'I wonder what was eating him.'

'He was probably just needing his coffee,' Jill replied, as

she picked up the dirty cups and headed into the tiny kitchen to wash them. She knew he'd been building up to asking her to the ball, and now that she'd accepted, the tension had left him. Was he really that sensitive? She was far more used to the brusque, all macho, blunt-spoken Aussie males that she'd met at school and at University. She realised Andrew did find it difficult to express his emotions. Were all Scotsmen like that? The stiff upper lip type? She'd thought that was more an English trait, from what she'd heard. She decided to ask Dorothy.

'Can I pick your brains?' she asked, seating herself again at her desk. Dorothy was filing some papers.

'What I've left of them. I can't say I'll be able to help much, but fire away.'

'Scotsmen,' Jill began. 'Are they really as buttoned-up about their feelings as they appear to be?'

'Where did you get that impression?' Dorothy asked. 'How many Scotsmen have you met?'

'Not that many. But compared to Sam O'Connor and Grigor, the ballet dancer that I met at the reception, they don't seem to show their feelings much. No, that's not quite true.' She stopped and thought for a moment. 'They do show their anger and annoyance and frustration, but when it comes to romance and affection and love…' Jill tailed off when she saw a smile on Dorothy's face.

'You've noticed.' Dorothy laughed. 'The highest praise a Scotsman will offer is to say that something's not bad. Or rather, no' bad, as we say here. His football team will win, and he'll say they played no' bad. You're all dressed up and looking great, and he'll tell you that you look no' bad. The sun is streaming down and it's scorching hot, and he'll say the weather's no' bad.'

Jill laughed, too.

'And,' Dorothy continued, 'if you're waiting for your

man to tell you he loves you, the sun will have burnt itself out before he manages to get his mouth round "I love you".'

'They can't all be as bad as that,' Jill remonstrated. 'There must be some who are able to show their feelings, and fall in love with you, and… and romance you.'

'Maybe the younger ones are better at it now,' she said. 'When my husband proposed to me, it was to point out that there was a nice wee house for sale round the corner from where I lived, and did I fancy living in it? So, I took it that he wanted to get married, and I was right. We've been together for almost twenty years now, so something's worked right.'

'You're so lucky,' Jill said, as she flipped through the phone book for a number. 'Not many people manage that nowadays.' But that's what I'd like, she thought, her fingers riffling through the pages. Someone to marry, to have a family with, and to know I'll be spending the rest of my life with them. She imagined what Andrew would look like at, say 64; if he would be grey and distinguished, or if he would have put weight on, or have kept his trim figure, would he have wrinkles around his eyes?

In her mind, she could see his face, see them both walking hand-in-hand, with kids running along in front of them, maybe pushing a pram, then later, all out in the country riding bicycles, watching the kids graduate, marry, produce grandchildren.

The pictures ran through her mind and she lived them in her thoughts, imagining her future life, partly in Scotland, partly in Australia. She'd take the kids to Australia often so that her mother could get to know her grandchildren well, so that they would know the country their mum came from, and she'd tell them the story of how she came to meet their dad.

'Jill!' The sound of Andrew's voice dissolved the dream. 'That's the third time I've called you. Are you sure you're ok?'

'What?' Jill said, blinking as she came back to reality. 'Sorry. Yes, what was it?'

'Come into the office. There's a mistake in the expenses for the party that I need to check out with you. I think you've counted some things in twice.'

As she rose, Dorothy raised her eyebrows and turned back to her own work. Jill picked up her pad and followed Andrew into his office, closing the door behind her.

18

In the flat that evening, Jill clicked on her emails and watched as one from Linda came up. She'd read it before she went to bed, but she had been far too tired to think about replying to it. She was emotionally drained from the roller coaster of emotions she'd experienced over the weekend, from the highs of Andrew's kiss and the day spent out in the fresh air, to the lows of his coolness and backing away from her. And worst of all, this afternoon's scolding for not having the expenses completely accurate and up-to-date. He'd rounded it all off by telling her that Margery's daughter would be coming out of hospital soon, and that Margery would be back at work in a week or two.

'That will suit me fine,' Jill had told him as she left the office. She'd buried herself in work for the rest of the day, and come home tired, and down, and with a headache threatening. All she wanted to do after her meal was to go to bed and forget about everything, even the forthcoming Caledonian Ball. Especially the Caledonian Ball. Did she really want to go to it with a man whose character changed with the wind? Who could be charming, kind and solicitous one moment, and a nagging, bad-tempered perfectionist the next? And furthermore, if she was going to be out of work in a couple of weeks, then she didn't want to spend any of her hard-earned savings on titivating herself just to please him. As it was, with the job finishing so soon, she wouldn't be able to afford much of a trip unless the Misses MacDonald at Elite Employment could find her something else.

She clicked on Linda's email. Her aunt had been travelling again – this time to Darwin and to the northern national parks. She sounded as if she was having a wonderful time, camping under the stars, keeping a wary eye out for the big crocs in the creeks, learning about the indigenous culture, and no doubt collecting masses of material for her next books. Then she said,

Did you and Andrew make it to the Tattoo? I do hope so. He and Nicola always used to take me with them, and then come back for supper to the flat. It was always such fun and a great night out.

Jill read those lines again. Who was Nicola? And when did she disappear off the scene? Or was she still around? Was that what Andrew had been about to confess to her this morning before Dorothy interrupted them?

Jill switched off the computer and headed for bed. But instead of a good night's restful sleep without even a dream to disturb it, she tossed and turned, threw off the bedclothes and rolled across the bed in a vain attempt to sleep. Her head was filled with Nicola and her relationship with Andrew. What had she meant to him? Did he still think of her? Was she beautiful? Where did she work? Were they married? Engaged? She couldn't provide answers to any of those questions, though her brain came up with many possible ones which whirled and twisted in her head until she was glad when she saw the sky brightening and realised that morning was near.

The next few days were hectic. Andrew seemed determined to tie up every single loose end before taking his break at the cottage, and he kept Jill busy every moment she was in the office. She even worked late one night to double check that all was completed and spot on, as she didn't want another telling off from him.

It looked as if the Caledonian Ball was to be her swan song. Margery would be taking over again, and Andrew would be heading north to the Trossachs for his holiday. When Jill and Dorothy did have time to exchange news and pleasantries, Dorothy always turned the subject to the ball. She had a new dress, and kept on at Jill to go out and buy one, too. But Jill was adamant.

'What's the point of me buying a dress I'll only wear once?' she said. 'Anyway, it won't fit in my suitcase and it won't be any use to me when I go travelling. I'm not likely to suddenly find myself going to another big ball in the middle of the Highlands, am I?'

Dorothy had to agree with Jill's argument. 'Linda's wardrobe is crammed with dresses that I could borrow. She must have gone to numerous grand affairs, by the looks of them.'

Dorothy laughed. 'She's quite a character, your aunt, isn't she? She and Andrew always got on so well together.'

'Did you meet Nicola?' It was out before Jill could think. She hadn't a clue that she was about to say that, and bit her lip as she waited for Dorothy's answer.

Dorothy hesitated. 'Yes, I did,' she said. 'How did you find out about her?'

Just then, Andrew's door opened. Jill flushed. Had he overheard what she'd said? What would he think? But he obviously hadn't, because he came out with a smile on his face.

'Jill, can you dance?' he asked.

She nodded.

'No, I mean. Can you do a Dashing White Sergeant? An Eightsome Reel? The Gay Gordons?'

Jill looked blank.

'These are the dances we do at the ball,' he explained. 'You need to know them. Come on, let's get started.' With that, he began pushing back the desks and chairs to clear a space in the centre of the reception area. 'We'll begin with the Dashing White Sergeant. We need three for that, so up you get, Dorothy.'

Andrew took both their hands and led them through the steps. 'Right,' he ordered, 'pretend we're in a circle of six. Eight steps round to the left, then eight to the right. Now, I set first to you, Jill – *pas de bas* – Jill!'

'What?' she said. 'What's that?'

'It's one of the basic steps,' he explained. 'Look, like this.'

The rest of the afternoon was spent prancing around the office in a semblance of Scottish country dancing. Dorothy and Andrew knew all the dances and tried to keep Jill on the right track, but they were forever having to turn her to face the right way or pulling her back into line with them.

Eventually, Dorothy collapsed into a chair, the tears streaming down her face with laughter at Jill's latest effort.

'Oh dear, Jill, you'll need to practise with Andrew every night if you're going to know the dances well enough to do them at the ball without making a muck of it all.'

Andrew and Jill looked at each other. She could see from Andrew's face that he was as keen on the idea as she was. The last thing she wanted to do was to spend every evening with him as well as all day in the office. If she was leaving the job in a week or two, then she'd better cool off towards him so that she was ready to move on. And she'd keep away from old drunk men on park benches. Why had those few minutes so unsettled her? That old man had put an idea into her head that wasn't there before, and she was having the devil of a job removing it.

'I'm going to be pretty busy in the evenings,' she said. 'I want to plan out my trip and I need to read up on all the places I want to visit.'

Andrew nodded, a serious look on his face. 'Good idea,' he said. 'You don't want to miss out on anything important.'

'Oh, come on,' Dorothy said. 'Surely you can fit in a spare half-hour's dancing at some point? We can't have Jill messing up a set by going the wrong way or forgetting what comes next.'

'If the dancing's taken that seriously, then I don't think I want to go,' Jill said, turning to Andrew. 'You'd be better off taking someone who knows all the dances. I'd just be a liability.'

Andrew seemed to be giving due consideration to this, but Dorothy burst in, 'Don't be ridiculous. Of course, you must come. You'll be fine, you'll see. We'll keep you straight.'

'No, really, Andrew.' She looked him straight in the eye. 'I don't actually mind if I don't go. Please feel free to ask someone else.' Like Nicola, her thoughts went. Half of her wanted him to agree with her and let her off the hook, but another little voice in her was doing its best to will him to insist that she accompany him.

'Well, if that's how you feel,' Andrew began.

'Don't be silly, Andrew,' Dorothy broke in. 'Jill's got to come to the ball. She deserves to. She's worked hard and fitted in well, and it will be something for her to remember about Scotland when she goes home. Anyway,' she finished, 'Margery's dying to meet her. She'd never forgive you if you took someone else.'

'I guess you'll have to keep up the practising, then,' said Andrew as he headed back into his office.

19

S o Jill did. Mostly with Dorothy, however. Every lunchtime, after a quick coffee and a sandwich, the two of them danced up and down the reception area. Once she got the hang of the basic steps, Jill quickly picked up the dances and even wrote down a page of steps, and sketches of the moves and sequences for her to memorise at home. While her evening meal was cooking, she would run through them all in Linda's lounge until she was pretty certain she knew them.

The next step was to decide what to wear. One evening, she spent a couple of pleasurable hours going through Linda's wardrobe and trying on some of her dresses. She had emailed her aunt for advice as to what would be suitable.

The reply came from an internet café somewhere near Cape Tribulation.

I'm delighted that you're going to the ball with Andrew. You will make a beautiful couple. He always looks so handsome in his full Highland outfit – the kilt and sporran, the silk shirt and waistcoat, the black velvet jacket and plaid. He's got the build for a kilt, I always think. It's not every man that can carry it off, but he looks particularly dishy in it.

Now, as to what you should wear. With your colouring, I suggest you try the dark green chiffon which you won't have noticed, as it's in a box under the bed.

There was more than one box under Linda's bed. 'The bed doesn't need any legs,' Jill muttered to herself. 'It's resting on all this stuff.'

Eventually, after opening up several boxes containing sheaves of paper (unpublished manuscripts probably, Jill surmised), hats in all shapes and sizes, and stacks of ornaments and bric-a-brac, Jill found the dress. Before she'd even looked at it properly, she knew she'd look good in it. The colour enhanced her eyes and set off her tanned skin perfectly. The cut flowed over her figure, lingering where her curves showed and giving a subtle glimpse of a cleavage. She would be more than a match for a kilted Andrew.

She hung the dress on the door of the wardrobe to let it air and to allow any crushes and wrinkles to iron out. Every time she went into the bedroom, a shiver of excitement ran through her when she saw it. Had Andrew taken Nicola to the ball? What had she worn? And would Jill look as good as she had? Or even better?

ACROSS THE LANDING, Andrew had taken out his kilt and jacket from its protective plastic cover and inspected it for any stains or marks. There was still time to send it off to be cleaned before the ball. When had he last worn it? Where had he been? He grinned when he remembered. He and Linda Naismith had gone to a wedding of a mutual friend at St Giles Cathedral in the Royal Mile, with the reception at a country house hotel just outside the city. The two of them had danced the night away at the ceilidh after the meal, whirling and birling till their feet were aching and they were exhausted. Linda had been great company, her sense of humour and funny anecdotes entertaining the table to which they'd been allocated.

Then his smile faded. He had originally bought the kilt and jacket to wear at Nicola's brother's wedding several years ago. The kilt was MacCallum tartan – soft shades of dark blue and green checks, with thin stripes of black and grey crisscrossing up and down. Nicola had worn a cerise coloured dress and jacket, which had clashed horribly with it.

That had been their first really big argument, and the beginning of the end as a couple. She had wanted him to change the tartan to something that would more closely match her outfit, while he had remonstrated that there never was a tartan that resembled the wild red she'd chosen. Anyway, he'd argued, did she intend to wear that colour to every event they attended, or should Andrew buy a new kilt for each occasion so that he wouldn't clash with her? And because of the cost of a kilt, they would have to limit their outings to one a year.

Now, he recalled his sarcasm with embarrassment. Really, the argument wasn't just about the kilt; it was the last straw in a long line of petty differences which had built up without resolution until they had exploded in a torrent of angry words and accusations, leaving both of them shaken and fearful of their future together.

He had intended asking Nicola to marry him up to that point, but things were never the same again and the moment had gone.

He hung up the kilt and jacket, unfolded the plaid which he would pin over his shoulder, and thought about the woman who would partner him to this year's ball. Was he mad to let her go so easily? Was he letting an opportunity slip through his fingers? He was noted for seizing every chance that came his way in business, so why not in his personal life? Because it would affect his business; it would mean that his whole attention would no longer be in building up his portfolio, in developing his contacts, in proving to others the extent of his business acumen.

His company, which he had been in the process of setting up just as he and Nicola were splitting, had been his lifesaver. He had thrown his energies into it, spending twenty-three out of twenty-four hours in thinking about it, working on it, nursing it along until it took on a life of its own. He had not allowed himself to grieve over the break-up; not allowed himself to show how deeply he had been hurt; not allowed anyone to peek beneath the stern, serious demeanour he had adopted as cover for his true feelings.

And now he was in danger of it happening all over again, of falling madly for someone who wouldn't last the course, who would disappear just as he came to depend emotionally on her. Jill was only over here temporarily, and she would return to Australia at the end of it. He remembered clearly her chatting to that Ukrainian ballet dancer, Grigor whats-it, her eyes glinting and sparkling under his attentions.

Twenty-seven was too young for career women nowadays to be thinking of settling down. Andrew was sure that, like many of them around her age, she would want to play the field for a bit longer, have the freedom that being a young, single woman with good job prospects in teaching and a steady income would bring, and not be bothered about finding Mr. Right and becoming a mother to his children.

Andrew knew only too well that he was ready for just such a scenario. Unfortunately, Jill didn't fit the job spec. So, in love as in business, he would have to let her go. He could be ruthless enough in the world of commerce, so why couldn't he be equally so when it came to his own heart? He would take her to the ball, leave her behind when he went off to Margery's cottage, and she would have left the job by the time he came back. That still left the small matter of her residing across the landing in Linda's flat, but if she stuck to her plans of setting off to tour Scotland, then he wouldn't see her there either.

In the meantime, he would be polite and mannerly towards her, cool yet reasonably friendly, so that their evening together at the ball would pass pleasantly enough for both of them. They would dance together and mingle with the crowd of friends he knew would be there, share the delicious supper served halfway through, and then he'd bring her back to her flat and wish her goodnight. His emotions would be firmly under control, and no-one would guess that she could send his heart rate soaring with a glance from under her long lashes or with one of her quirky grins.

He packed the kilt into its bag and laid it out to remind him to drop it off at the specialist cleaners. He wanted it to be in pristine condition. Nobody was going to be able to say he wasn't putting on a show for his partner. He just hoped that Dorothy was guiding Jill about what she should wear. He had overheard Jill vehemently declaring she wasn't spending her hard-earned cash on something she would only wear once, so she would wear one of her aunt's outfits. And while he admired her common sense, he was concerned that she might choose one of Linda's more outrageous and highly-coloured creations. Hopefully, not one in cerise, at any rate.

20

On Saturday, a week before the ball, Jill was outside her flat, sweeping the landing and stairs. It had been in Linda's instructions that she should sweep the stairs once a week, but Jill hadn't done it since the day after the party, and her conscience was bothering her. Iris upstairs was dedicated to the cleaning of her part of the stair every week, and Jill suspected she also swept Linda and Andrew's landing as well.

So that morning, Jill resurrected the brush and shovel from the broom cupboard, and was energetically gathering the dust and debris together when she heard the outer door open and close, and footsteps coming towards the stairs. She leant over the balustrade and recognised the top of Andrew's head.

Blast! she thought. She really didn't want to see him, especially dressed in her old jeans and t-shirt and wielding the brush. But she couldn't just stop in the middle and run and hide in her flat, so she made herself look as busy as possible while Andrew's footsteps climbed ever closer.

She heard him stop as he saw her, and then continue

upwards. She kept her eyes firmly on her sweeping, and banged and clattered the brush and shovel so that she could pretend not to have heard him then be surprised to see him at the top of the stairs.

But her face, she was sure, gave her away. He looked as embarrassed as she felt, as he stood there with a long plastic suit bag over his shoulder.

'You're busy,' he eventually said.

She nodded as she swept aside the debris so that he could walk across to his front door. 'Linda told me I should sweep the landing and stairs every week, but I've been a bit remiss about it, so I thought I'd better make the effort.'

Andrew roared with laughter. 'Linda is a one,' he said. 'I don't think I ever saw her sweeping the stairs properly. Occasionally, she'd brush the dust over the edge so that it fell down to the lower landing, but actually shovelling it up? Well, I don't know that she did that too often.'

Jill leant on the brush, a wry expression crossing her features. 'You know she'll deny that. She'll swear blind she faithfully swept up every week so it's up to me to keep up her high standards.'

Andrew bent a bit closer to Jill. 'She writes fiction,' he whispered. 'She makes up stories all the time. She says what she likes and believes every word of it. She doesn't let anything stand in the way of a good story.'

Jill had to smile. 'Yes, that's Linda. Mum always used to say that her sister's hobby as a child was embroidery, and I never understood quite what she meant because she never actually sewed anything. But I suppose it's a necessary skill of a writer to be able to create stories out of nothing much.'

Andrew shifted the bag to his other shoulder.

'Is that your kilt?' Jill asked.

He nodded. 'I've just had it cleaned and pressed, so it's looking good. Would you like to see it?'

'Yes, please,' she said.

She left the brush leaning against the landing wall and followed Andrew into his flat. He went into his bedroom, laid the bag on the bed and unzipped it. Jill gasped when she saw the kilt and the matching black jacket and waistcoat.

'It's almost a perfect match for my dress,' she said. 'Linda suggested a dark green one, and it's the same tone as your kilt. Let me bring it through and we'll see.'

She dashed off to her flat, leaving Andrew with a relieved smile on his face. So, it wasn't going to be some cerise creation, after all.

In a moment she was back, cradling the soft chiffon in her arms. She laid it on the bed next to the kilt.

'Perfect,' Andrew said. 'It's a very close match. I think we're going to look pretty good at this ball.'

'I hope so,' said Jill. 'I was worried you wouldn't like what I'd decided on.'

'I once went to the ball with someone in a dreadful bright red outfit,' he said. 'We clashed all evening.'

And we clashed verbally as well, he thought to himself. He couldn't believe he'd mentioned the incident to Jill; hopefully she wouldn't ask any searching questions as to his partner's identity. He didn't feel up to revealing his thoughts on that.

Jill, meantime, was stroking the fabric of the kilt and jacket. 'It's quite heavy,' she said. 'Don't you get very warm in it?'

'It's pure wool,' he replied. 'It's much cooler than you think, and the natural fabric lets your skin breathe, unlike synthetics.'

He lifted up a sports bag from the side of the bed and

opened it. 'The accessories are in here,' he said, taking out a furry round object with silver chains. 'This is the sporran,' he explained. 'It's a kind of purse which loops onto the kilt and hangs down the front; this is the MacCallum crest on it.'

Jill took the sporran and stroked the fur. There were three tassels on the front, attached to the silver band across the top where the crest was inscribed. 'It's beautiful,' she said, letting the silver chains run through her fingers.

'And this is the sgian dubh.' Andrew pulled out a small silver dagger with a decorated hilt, encased in a leather sheath, and handed it to her. 'The family crest is on it, too.' Jill peered at the silver shield engraved with the Scottish saltire and with four deers' heads in between – the same design as on the sporran.

'Why do you have a dagger?' she asked, carefully pulling it from its sheath. Its steel blade glinted, and the dark blue stone set in the top of the hilt reflected myriad crystals of light.

'In the old days, it was for protection. We wear them tucked into the top of the long socks so that they're handy if ever they were needed to defend ourselves. But it's purely decorative nowadays.'

'It's beautiful, if pretty lethal,' said Jill, handing it back to him.

'And there's also the plaid brooch,' Andrew said, reaching into the bag again and bringing out a dark blue velvet case which he opened. Inside was a round pewter brooch with four dark blue stones surrounding what Jill now recognised as being the MacCallum crest. She lifted it out, and was surprised at its weight.

'It holds the plaid on to my shoulder,' explained Andrew. 'So that it doesn't fly away when we're dancing.'

He took out a length of tartan to match his kilt. 'This is

the plaid, and the brooch holds it like this.' His hand touched Jill's as he took the brooch and showed her how it would clasp the cloth just below his left shoulder, leaving the rest of the plaid loose at his back.

She could scarcely pay attention, aware as she was of the tingling in her hand where his fingers had touched. The sooner she left the job and the flat, the better, she thought, as Andrew folded the plaid and laid it carefully back in the bag.

He looked up at her. 'Well,' he said, 'aren't you going to ask me?'

Jill looked flustered. 'Ask you what?'

'The question every woman wants to ask,' he replied with a grin. 'What do Scotsmen wear under their kilts?'

Jill smiled, too. 'Oh, that old chestnut,' she said as casually as she dared. Her mind was imagining all sorts of possible answers, none of which she was going to admit to. Let him think it had never crossed her mind and she wasn't all that interested in finding out. So, when she found herself saying, 'What do you wear?' she wished the floor could open up and take her home to Oz immediately.

'That's my secret,' he said, his eyes twinkling, 'though I hope the dancing doesn't get too energetic. Or that there's not a gale blowing on Saturday. You might just find out.'

Jill took a deep breath, lifted up her dress, and turned to go. 'Thanks for that,' she said. 'Cinderella had better get back to her sweeping.'

'I suppose Linda is your fairy godmother then,' he said, following her to the door. 'After all, she gave you the dress.'

Jill nodded. 'And are you auditioning for the role of the prince?' her eyebrows arched quizzically.

'I wish,' came the reply. 'More like Buttons, probably.'

She left him standing at his front door, a wistful look on his face.

21

For Jill, the day of the Caledonian Ball couldn't have been more perfect. It was a gentle late September Indian summer day, which bathed the city in a soft hazy light. She spent the morning at a beauty salon – the sole expense that she was prepared to rise to. While her hair was trimmed and washed and dried, so that it hung like a golden curtain around her features, her nails were polished and buffed and painted a soft pink. She felt pretty, and a match for any of Andrew's former partners, whoever they had been.

The previous day, she had spent tidying up her desk and leaving Post-it notes stuck all over the computer for Margery. Even though she hadn't been in the job long, Jill felt sad at finally going. Dorothy gave her a big hug and made her promise to keep in touch and tell her all about her trip around Scotland. Andrew had thanked her, and made arrangements to pick her up for the ball as if they were not about to say farewell.

She still hadn't decided exactly where or when she was going on her trip, but she knew it would be sooner rather than later. Meanwhile, on Monday morning, she was going to call on the Elite Employment Agency and the Misses MacDonald, to see if they had another job she could take for a short while. A change of scenery would do her good, and take her away from Andrew's disturbing presence.

But Andrew had been friendly and pleasant enough over the past week, and she was looking forward to spending the evening in his company. He seemed much more relaxed and at ease with himself now that the business was entering a quiet phase before the onslaught of the Christmas festivities. He's probably looking forward to his break at Margery's cottage, she told herself, as she'd watched him josh with Dorothy about a new hairstyle she'd appeared with. Jill couldn't have imagined him doing that a couple of weeks before.

She planned to be amicable and enjoy herself at the ball as if it didn't really matter that they might not see each other again. Changed days, she thought; not so long ago, the last thing she had wanted to do was to spend time with him.

So, it was with mixed feelings on Saturday evening that she slid the green chiffon dress over her shoulders and let it shimmy down her body. She slipped on Linda's gold strappy shoes, and stood in front of the mirror. She had to admit that she did look good. Gone was the gauche Australian girl, out for adventure and fun in a new country. In her place stood a sophisticated young woman, ready to face whatever life could throw at her.

The last few weeks had taught her a lot about herself and her feelings, and she felt years older than that day she'd first set eyes on Andrew. He was no longer the arrogant, pushy, and rude character that she'd taken him for in the beginning, but a much more complex and intriguing person that she'd ever imagined. He had his faults like everyone else, but she liked him, if she was being honest. She liked him a great deal.

The doorbell rang exactly when Andrew said he would pick her up. He was punctual as always; another point in his favour. She sashayed and swished to the front door, feeling excited and pretty, and opened it. Prince Charming stood there, resplendent in his full Highland outfit. For a moment, she couldn't say anything, taken aback by the full-frontal assault on her senses.

'You look... you look... fabulous,' she finished lamely, other words failing her. And, indeed, he did. And he knew it. He glowed with masculinity, and pride, and confidence.

'You look fantastic yourself,' he said. 'Are you ready? Your pumpkin carriage awaits.'

He proffered his arm, and with a delighted smile, Jill allowed him to escort her down the stairs and into the waiting black cab. It was only a short journey to the grand hotel on Princes Street where the Caledonian Ball was being held. Already, guests were arriving, and the taxi driver had to wait as finely dressed women and kilted men were deposited at the front door by numerous cabs and private vehicles.

Andrew helped Jill out of the cab, and she stood and admired the elegant facade of the hotel while he paid off the taxi. Then, slipping her arm into his, they made their way into the grand foyer, where a uniformed commission-aire directed them up a sweeping staircase to the ballroom on the first floor.

Truly, Jill knew what Cinderella must have felt on entering the ballroom. Majestic chandeliers hung at inter-vals around the room, their crystals sending sparkles of light dancing across the ceiling. Rich crimson drapes hung at the tall windows, shielded by long white nets from the real world outside. Around the edges of the ballroom were tables set out for ten, each covered in pristine white damask cloth, and with a centrepiece of pale pink roses and white heather, tied with tartan ribbon. Waiters dressed in tartan waistcoats rushed between the tables and the bar, dispensing drinks with quiet efficiency.

Jill gasped when she saw the elegant and colourful dresses of the other women, many with tartan sashes across their shoulders. But it was the men who drew her attention. They were all in full Highland dress, a few wearing tartan trews rather than the kilt. It created a bright spectacle, the men for a change being as colourful as the women. There were green and blue tartans like Andrew's, bright red and green ones, purples and darker blues, lighter coloured ones with a predominance of white in the check, and even a couple of plain black kilts.

'The trendy set,' Andrew whispered in her ear, when Jill asked him about them. 'It's supposed to be very fashionable. But I prefer real tartan myself.'

As they made their way to their table, Andrew identified as many tartans as he could to Jill.

'The Royal Stewart, the Red Fraser, the Black Watch, don't know that one, the Dress Gordon, the Buchanan…'

An older couple were already seated at their table. 'Margery,' Andrew said, going up to the woman and kissing her on the cheek. 'It's good to see you again.' He shook hands with Tom, her husband, and then turned and introduced Jill to them.

Margery immediately hugged her. 'Lovely to meet you,' she said. 'And thank you for standing in for me, and doing so well too. She's done a wonderful job, hasn't she, Andrew? Not many people could have stepped in as you did, and arranged everything so perfectly.'

Jill didn't look at Andrew as she thought about the near fiasco of the party. Just as well Margery didn't know about that or she wouldn't have been so effusive in her praises.

'Hello, folks,' Dorothy said, as she and her husband, Norman, arrived. 'Jill, you look sensational. Is that one of Linda's outfits? I didn't know her taste could be so good.'

'It looks a lot better on Jill than it would on Linda,' said Margery. 'It needs a youthful skin and figure to carry it off, don't you think? It really is the ideal dress for Jill. Did Linda ever wear it, I wonder?'

'Now, ladies,' said Andrew. 'Enough talk of clothes and absent friends. Let's have an enjoyable evening and, just so you know, I've booked the first dance with Jill. You gentlemen,' he nodded at Norman and Tom, 'will just have to wait your turn.' He lifted a couple of glasses of champagne from a waiter's tray and gave one to Jill. 'Here's to a great night,' he said, raising his glass. 'And to a beautiful woman,' he whispered, as they settled themselves round the table.

And it was an unforgettable evening. Jill danced virtually every dance, managing the steps not too badly, and carrying off her mistakes with an aplomb which came from knowing she looked good. And when Andrew whirled her around the floor in a reel or a *Schottische*, she felt that life could not get any better than it was. She lived for the moment, and it showed in her face, her eyes sparkling and her smile radiant.

Andrew looked entranced by her. He was clearly enjoying the feel of her lithe young body in his as they danced, aware of the admiring glances of the men as he spun Jill across the floor, of the envious glances of the women as she outshone them in looks, and vitality, and joie de vivre.

'What a handsome couple they are,' Dorothy remarked

to Margery, as Andrew and Jill waltzed past. 'It's almost as if they were made for each other.'

'I just hope, for her sake, he's finally over Nicola,' said Margery. 'For a while there, it looked as if nobody could replace her.'

Dorothy bent towards her colleague. 'It's a pity you're able to come back to work. You couldn't arrange to have a nasty viral infection, could you? Give them a bit more time to sort things out?'

Margery laughed. 'You're forgetting he's staying in my cottage all next week, so even if I were ill, it wouldn't do any good as Andrew is on holiday. But, remember, they live across the landing from each other. They can carry on seeing each other that way.'

'What do you think the chances are?' said Dorothy. 'Shall we have a wee bet on it?'

'You'll be wanting to rush out and buy a fancy hat for the wedding next,' said Margery with a smile. 'Don't count your chickens, as the old saying goes. Let's just wait and see.'

AT SUPPER, Andrew introduced Jill around his many friends and acquaintances. They all seemed pleased to see him looking so happy.

'Back to your old self,' Jill heard one of them say, as he patted Andrew on the shoulder. 'Too long "all work and no play", eh?'

Jill enjoyed meeting them all, and chatted easily to them. They were a cross-section of Edinburgh folk from various walks of life, and all with interesting tales to tell or experiences to relate. The laughter rang out often, as some incident was embellished in the telling and turned into a humorous anecdote. Jill was almost sorry when the dancing started again, and the groups broke up and took to the floor.

Midnight came, and she was still dancing with her handsome prince. Her feet ached in Linda's shoes, but she wasn't stopping for anything. So, it was much later – after *Auld Lang Syne* had been sung with gusto, ending up with everyone holding hands in a circle and marching into the centre of the floor and out again – that she and Andrew made their way out of the hotel towards home. They had planned to take a taxi, but so had everyone else, so the street outside was empty of black cabs or transport of any kind.

'We can either wait for a taxi or we can walk,' Andrew said.

'Let's walk,' replied Jill. 'It's not far, it's dry, and my feet couldn't be any more painful than they are.'

Hand-in-hand, the two of them set off to climb the hill leading to the Canongate. Jill was full of the night's experience, and babbled on happily about it all until she was aware of the growing silence of her companion. She stopped talking and looked at him. He was staring straight ahead, his lips tight closed, and that tic throbbing in his jaw again. What had she said? What had she done?

'Andrew…' she began.

'Don't start,' he said in a strangled voice. 'Just keep walking.'

'What have I done?' she cried. 'What on earth have I said to make you change like this? Why won't you talk to me?'

Andrew refused to look at her, but shook his hand free and walked ahead. After a moment, Jill ran after him and grabbed his arm.

'Stop right there,' she said. 'I deserve an explanation for your behaviour. As far as I know, I've behaved correctly, talked to your friends, danced all night, not disgraced myself or embarrassed you, so what's wrong?'

'It's not you, it's me,' he said, still averting his eyes. 'I'm sorry. I don't mean to be rude, but I can't handle this. Let's just get home and say goodnight, and tomorrow I'll be off on holiday.'

'And that's it?' Jill's anger was rising. 'No "Thanks for all your hard work. Thanks for your company tonight. I've enjoyed your friendship, so keep in touch."? Simply clear off now and we'll pretend we never met. We'll pretend it all never happened. We'll pretend it's all been a dream. More like a nightmare, actually.

'I've never met a more mercurial, arrogant, self-centred man as you, and frankly, if I never see you again, it will be the best thing that's happened in this sorry state of affairs. I couldn't care less if you disappear out of my life right now!'

And with that, she grasped a handful of her chiffon dress and began running down the cobbled street towards Linda's flat.

'Jill!' she heard Andrew shout. 'Jill! Stop that! It's—'

But she didn't hear the rest of his warning, as her feet slipped from under her and she went crashing down onto the cobbles, her ankle twisting sharply as Linda's high heels slewed sideways. It seemed to happen in slow motion. One moment she was running, the next she was in the air, tilting forwards and heading for the cobbles.

She tried to put out her hands to save herself and break her fall, but her head thumped against the stones and she was momentarily stunned. When she came to, Andrew was beside her, his mobile phone to his ear.

'I've called an ambulance,' he told her. 'Don't move. Just lie still.' He slipped off his jacket and laid it across her shoulders. Suddenly, she couldn't stop shivering, as a chill swept over her. She felt dizzy and slightly nauseous, and her head hurt. Some late-night stragglers had joined them, all keen to help and offer advice, so it was with some relief that they heard the wail of the ambulance approaching.

It was only when she was being gently lifted onto a stretcher that her ankle pained her, and she realised that she had hurt it quite badly. Please don't let it be broken, she said to herself, as the ambulance men checked her over.

22

Dawn was breaking over the city when a taxi disgorged a couple in evening dress outside a building in the Canongate. Jill was clutching a set of crutches, while Andrew tried to both support her and carry a single strappy gold sandal.

'Right, Cinderella,' he said. 'Let's try to get you upstairs.'

The wait in the Accident and Emergency department of the nearest hospital had been long, as various more urgent cases had been dealt with. Andrew and Jill had created quite a stir among the other patients, none of whom were as finely dressed as they were.

'See what happens when you do an energetic Highland Fling!' one wag with a bad cut over an eye had commented.

Eventually, when Jill was examined by a doctor, the bump on her head was pronounced sore but nothing to worry about apart from the unsightly lump, and her ankle was strapped up with instructions to rest it as much as possible for several weeks while the torn ligaments healed.

Jill was relieved that no great harm had been done, but standing outside the entrance to their building, she began to realise the implications of her injury and having to use crutches. How on earth was she going to negotiate a spiral staircase?

Andrew was also aware of the problem, because he handed the gold shoe to Jill then swept her up in his arms. Crutches flailing and striking off the banisters and the wall, they made their way slowly up the stairs to the landing.

'Phew,' he said somewhat ungallantly, as he put her down outside her door, 'I wouldn't like to do that too often.'

He opened her door with her key and was about to carry her over the threshold when Jill poked a crutch at him and said, 'No, I'll walk. I've got to learn how to use these dratted things, and the sooner the better.'

She hobbled into the bedroom, threw herself rather inelegantly onto the bed, and let the crutches drop on the floor. She was exhausted, yet she doubted if she would sleep. It had been an emotional night, what with the enjoyment of the actual ball, through Andrew's sudden coolness, and then her fall and the subsequent visit to A&E. Andrew couldn't have been more caring and solicitous, and seemed genuinely concerned for her. Jill couldn't fathom his abrupt changes of mood towards her. What was behind it all? Did he care for her or not?

He brought in a glass of water and set it on the bedside table.

'I'll put my number in your phone so you can buzz me if you need anything,' he said. 'Linda left me a spare key, so I can let myself in. In the meantime, let's get you into bed and you'll feel better after a few hours' sleep.'

'I can manage fine,' Jill said, sitting upright. 'I don't need any help. You get some shut-eye yourself. I'm sure you must be tired. And,' she continued, 'you want an early start to your holiday, don't you?'

Andrew looked at the floor. 'We'll see about that,' he mumbled. 'Are you sure you're ok?' His eyes at last met hers. 'Can I get you anything else?'

Jill shook her head and tried to smile. 'No. Thanks for everything. I'll be fine. Goodnight.'

Andrew nodded at her and made his way to the door. 'Goodnight then,' he said.

Jill listened as the front door opened and closed, and his footsteps crossed the landing to his flat.

'Have a good holiday,' she whispered, as a tear trickled down her cheek.

DESPITE HER MISGIVINGS, as soon as she got herself into her pyjamas and climbed into bed, she fell sound asleep. So, she was startled to waken suddenly with the sun streaming in through the windows and the sound of the heavy traffic struggling its slow way up the street. What else had she heard? She had become used to the noises of the front-facing bedroom, so what had wakened her?

The bedroom door opened, and Andrew entered carrying a tray.

'Sorry, I didn't mean to waken you,' he said, setting the tray down on space which he cleared on a chair. Jill was amazed to find that it was set for breakfast – *her* breakfast.

'What time is it?' she asked, sitting up and wrapping the bedclothes around her, conscious that her extremely practical and comfortable pyjamas were not particularly flattering.

'It's just gone eleven,' Andrew replied. 'I've made you coffee, or would you have preferred tea?'

'What? No, I mean yes, that's fine.' She leant forward

as he proceeded to plump up her pillows and arrange them so that she could lean back on them while she ate. Was this really happening? Was the great Andrew MacCallum-Blair doing a Florence Nightingale with her?

'Why haven't you left yet?' she blurted out, as he placed the tray on her knees. 'You're supposed to be heading for the Trossachs.'

'I couldn't leave you to fend for yourself,' he said, not meeting her gaze. 'You can't manage on your own with those things.' He pointed to the crutches, which lay on the floor where she'd dropped them before clambering into bed.

'Yes, I can,' Jill said through a mouthful of cereal. 'Of course I can manage.'

'You can't get up and down the stairs,' Andrew said.

'Well, I can ask Iris to pick up some things for me.'

'She's gone to London to stay with her daughter for a few days. You'd starve before she got back.'

'I could open the window and shout across to the coffee shop,' Jill suggested frantically. She didn't want to be responsible for Andrew not getting the break he so desperately needed. And anyway, she wasn't all that keen on him finding out the messier aspects of her character. She just hoped she'd put her panties in the dirty wash and not left them lying about, as she was often known to do.

'Don't be silly. I've got the week off, so I may as well do things for you until you're back on your feet.'

'But what about the cottage?' she wailed. 'It's a waste not to make use of it when you've got the chance.'

'That's true,' Andrew said with a beam that lit up his features. 'We could both go.'

23

The black Mercedes purred its way through the glen, pine trees on either side shutting out the watery sun and casting a gloom over the road. It mirrored exactly what Jill was feeling; dark, gloomy thoughts about the wisdom of what she was doing. It would only end in heart-break, and tears, and arguments, and things being said that they both would regret. So, why was she sitting in the back seat of Andrew's car, her damaged ankle propped up on cushions, and her luggage and her crutches stowed in the boot?

A week in a small Highland cottage, miles from anywhere, with only Andrew for company was a sure-fire recipe for disaster. Particularly with her dependent on him for help. She had been lying when she'd said she'd manage fine on her own at the flat. She couldn't have. A visit to the bathroom, when she'd almost fallen and cracked her head on the wash-basin, had shown all too clearly the necessity for some help around her, even if only for a couple of days until she became more confident on her crutches and the pain in her ankle had lessened.

So, now here she was, being driven to Margery's cottage to spend a week under its roof with full-on, undiluted Andrew. How was she going to stand it? What if he had one of his huffy turns when he could barely speak to her, never mind share an evening with her? She hoped and hoped that there was a pub nearby where he could go as often as possible, so that they could get out of each other's way in the evenings. And if he went for very long walks during the day, that too would mean several hours when they wouldn't be together. What about shopping? Could she send him off on long convoluted trips to the nearest town to buy whatever items she could claim were necessities?

'We're just coming into Callander. We'll stop there for a coffee.'

'Ok.' She would be glad of the break and the chance for some fresh air. The warmth of the car was lulling and, after the emotional events of the previous night, Jill had to fight to keep her eyes from closing.

The car slowed as it entered the small country town. From the number of little shops all tartan-bedecked and with the Scottish Saltire or the Lion Rampant flying outside, Jill deduced that it was geared for tourists. Indeed, a luxury coach was disgorging a stream of Japanese, who headed for the shops and the numerous tea-rooms and cafés along the main street. Outside each shop were racks of postcards and tea towels, stands of decorated mugs and Scotty dogs, dolls in Highland dress and miniature bagpipes. Andrew drove slowly on until they had almost left the town. Then he turned down a narrow alley, which opened out into a parking area at the rear of a tea-room.

'They make great scones here,' he said, opening the back door to help Jill out. 'All sorts of flavours: cheese, treacle, fruit, cinnamon. And you can have them with jam or cream, or both,' he added with a grin.

With a struggle, Jill extricated herself from the back seat. She felt light-headed and was glad to lean against the car door while Andrew brought out her crutches. Together, they hobbled into the tea-room. The waitress rushed to remove chairs and tables to ensure a clear path to an empty table, while the customers viewed their progress with interest, and one or two even smiled a greeting. At last, Jill sat down, and Andrew took her crutches and tucked them into a corner out of the way.

'Everything's such an effort,' she said. 'I'm sorry.'

'You were the one who wanted to be left alone like Greta Garbo,' said Andrew. 'I can't imagine how on earth you thought you were going to manage.'

Neither did Jill, but she wasn't going to admit as much. Nor did she want to annoy him, so she gave him what she hoped was a grateful smile. She couldn't help but notice the change in his demeanour since they'd left Edinburgh a couple of hours earlier. He was far more relaxed, obviously in holiday-mode, though he did keep checking his mobile. As Margery had said, he did need a break, but now here he was, lumbered with her like an albatross. I hope I'm much more mobile in a couple of days, she thought as she scanned the menu.

'Coffee,' Jill said to the waitress.

'Make that two, and a selection of scones.'

The scones were delicious, and the coffee was strong. They made short work of the plateful, and asked for extra coffee as well.

'I feel much better after that,' Jill said, wiping her mouth.

'That will keep us going till dinner,' said Andrew, as he helped her to her feet and guided her to the door. 'The pub across the road from the cottage does great food, so we can eat there.'

A pub across the road. With a bit of luck, he could spend quite a bit of time in there and she could read her book or watch TV. How boring, said a little voice inside her. Much more fun to joust with Andrew over a drink in the pub.

No can do, said the voice on her other shoulder. Keep out his way, and you'll be less likely to have an argument.

They drove on through dramatic scenery of rising hills covered with drifts of purple heather, and straying black faced sheep that ambled across the road, oblivious to the cars which had to slow down or stop while they meandered along.

'I don't know if we can see deer here,' Andrew said. 'It's the start of the rutting season, so the stags are probably high up in the hills looking for the hinds, and defending their group against young upstarts.'

Jill craned her head to try to see out of the window more clearly. From her position stretched out on the seat, she saw more of the clouds as they scudded by than anything else. She closed her eyes and, despite the coffee, fell asleep.

She woke to the noise of a car door opening. She sensed that they had stopped, and she raised her head to see where they were. A straggly climbing rose clung to a trellis against rough-hewn stone walls, and crawled its way round a small window frame. There was a last flush of pale pink roses angled towards the light, among which Jill saw bees and a couple of wasps searching for the sweet nectar.

'We're here,' said Andrew. 'Sit there till I open it up, and then we'll get you inside.'

She watched as he unlocked the front door and ducked to step inside. Idly, she wondered about the age of the cottage. To her Australian eyes, it looked a relic from the earliest times, far older than any buildings back home. If it had been in Oz, it would have been made into some national shrine to the earliest settlers. But here in Scotland, she mused, it was probably treated as just another ordinary two hundred-year-old building.

Andrew's head emerged first from the doorway. 'You're going to have a few bumps and bruises from that door before the week's up,' she said.

'Too right. Once we're inside, it's better. It's just the front door that's low. No doubt after the first few cracks on the forehead, I'll remember to duck.'

He helped manoeuvre Jill out of the car and through the front door. It was quite a business avoiding the lintel and taking a step down straight into the living room of the cottage. But, as Andrew had said, it was no problem to straighten up, and Jill felt more confident as she swung her crutches and hobbled over to the chintz-covered two-seater sofa in front of the fireplace. Thankfully, she sat down and looked about her.

It was a comfortable, homely room, but obviously a holiday cottage. The furniture was old and a bit shabby, there were cup rings and scratches on the coffee tables, and the curtains were faded where the sun had struck them. The fireplace was set ready to light, and a pile of logs sat in a scuttle by the side. Jill could imagine how cosy it would be to sit by the fire and watch the flames form pictures in her mind. Under any other circumstances, she would be thrilled to be here; this was what she had come to Scotland to experience, but Andrew's presence only served to disturb the tranquil mindset of the situation.

He was exploring the rest of the cottage, and she could hear his slightly off-key whistling as he inspected the other rooms. At least he's happy at the moment, she thought.

Just then, the whistling abruptly stopped. She listened as doors were opened and closed and his footsteps came and went, and eventually he came back to the living room.

'Houston, we have a problem,' he said, standing over Jill with his hands on his hips.

'What? Is something wrong?'

'There's only one bedroom. How on earth does Margery fit her entire family in here? I'll have to check if the pub has got a spare room.'

With that, he opened the front door and headed out, bumping his head on the lintel as he went. The front door banged shut to an outburst of words that Jill fortunately could only half hear, but could perfectly well understand the meaning of.

One bedroom. Had he known that before he brought her here? Probably not, if his reaction was anything to go by. Were there twin beds perhaps or just the one? Jill struggled to her feet and, grasping her crutches, set off to find out.

The first door she opened was a large walk-in cupboard full of fishing rods, Wellington boots, and heavy jackets. Obviously, Margery's family left their wet weather and fishing gear permanently at the cottage. Then the bathroom. Perfectly adequate, though she wondered how on earth she would manage to shower. Or have a bath. But she dismissed those problems from her mind and focused on the most immediate one.

She opened the door to the bedroom. It was a pleasant, airy room, again with mis-matched pieces of furniture, each with their own charm – and yes, a large double bed, covered in a patchwork quilt in tones of blues and greens. A number of pillows and cushions were piled up at the top, and she automatically reached out to straighten a small dark blue cushion embroidered in white and gold, which had slipped down. She patted it into place on top of the pillows and long white bolster, which stretched the width of the bed. Jill sighed as she gazed around. It was a room she would have delighted to have slept in, but on her own. Along the wall opposite the window was a large wooden wardrobe, obviously bulging with stuff. On an impulse, Jill reached over and opened it. Out tumbled a couple of fold-up camp beds and several inflatable airbeds.

The front door opened, and a yell of annoyance reverberated as Andrew yet again bumped his head. Oh dear, it didn't augur well.

'Where are you?' she heard, as he stomped along the passage to the bedroom. 'Didn't I tell you to stay put? You could hurt yourself.'

'You're the one who seems to be getting injured. That's twice you've bumped your head.'

'That's the last time,' he said, a rueful smile flitting across his face. 'I've learned my lesson now. Duck, duck, duck.'

Jill burst out laughing. 'So, how did you get on at the pub?'

Andrew shook his head. 'No room at the inn. There's a shooting party taken over the whole place, as well as every bed and breakfast between here and Callander.'

'Just as well I found these then,' she said, gesturing at the beds spilling out of the wardrobe.

'Oh, clever girl,' Andrew said. 'Pity you didn't find them sooner. It would have saved me a couple of cracks on the head from that blasted door frame.'

They made their way back to the living room, Andrew hovering behind her like an anxious mother cat. In turn, it made Jill even more unsteady on her crutches. She stopped.

'Please, Andrew, let me do this on my own. I've got to

learn. And if, like you, I bump myself, I'll remember better the next time.'

'We'll be like the walking wounded,' he said. 'Thank goodness the pub is just across the road. Which reminds me, if we want to eat there, we'd better get in ahead of the hunters or there won't be a lot left.'

'Let me freshen up and then we can go,' Jill said. 'Where's my bag?'

'What do you want out of it? You can't manage crutches as well as a brush or make-up.'

After various abortive attempts to get herself and her make-up and hairbrush into the bathroom, she gave up, sat on the sofa in the lounge, and let Andrew rummage around in her bag for what she needed. It felt overly personal to have him searching in amongst her spare underwear and clean t-shirts, and her face flushed at the thought of what else he might find. She had packed in such a hurry this morning, handing stuff to him to put in her bag.

All her plans to find another job before setting off on her travels were stymied by her silly accident, which had been her own fault. If she hadn't stomped off in such high dudgeon last night, she might not have fallen and hurt herself, and then she wouldn't have found herself stranded with Andrew in Margery's cottage. Her sensible self berated her for her stupidity, but there was now an ever-increasing other voice, secretly gleeful at her dependence on him. This was her big chance, it kept insisting; he had to take care of her whether she liked it or not, she was here alone with him, and yes, she did like him quite a lot. A whole lot, said that other voice. A great big gigantic lot.

'Ready?' Andrew said, as she quickly ran a comb through her hair and sprayed some of Chanel's Coco over herself. It had been a going away present from her mum, and its scent always reminded her of home.

Jill steadied herself on her crutches and tried to shoo Andrew out of the way. He walked in front of her, turning to watch as she negotiated her way around the furniture and headed for the door.

'Careful,' he cautioned. 'Not too fast.'

Crack! The side of his head met the lintel again.

Jill could only stand and listen as he questioned the parentage of the lintel, expressed his feelings as to what he'd like to do to it, and stuttered to a halt.

'Sorry,' he mumbled. 'Still haven't learned to duck.'

'You were paying far too much attention to me and not enough to where you were going,' Jill said. 'Let me make my own way and learn how to use these dratted things. If you keep protecting me, I'm never going to learn.'

Together, they attempted to make their way across the road to the pub. A journey that Jill would normally take a minute to do, seemed to take forever, especially when she couldn't move for laughing. Andrew stood in the middle of the road like a policeman, and watched for any oncoming cars while Jill tried to hobble across. But her crutches suddenly developed a will of their own and headed in different directions, while she stood on one leg, her injured ankle protectively tucked under her.

Try as she might, she couldn't coordinate her arms, legs, and crutches, so that she could move forward. Meanwhile, Andrew waited patiently in the middle of the road, arms outstretched ready to stop the traffic.

A man on a bike swooped round about him and nodded a greeting, and a milk tanker slowed to a halt only a couple of feet away. Meanwhile, Jill desperately tried to cross, her efforts reducing her to almost hysterical laughter.

'Pick her up, mate,' shouted the tanker driver through his open window. 'The cows will be standing with their legs crossed at this rate.'

Two cars coming the opposite way had stopped to watch the fun, and a group of men heading into the pub paused to see what would happen next.

Andrew started laughing, too, as he ran over to Jill and swooped her up in his arms. Crutches flailing, they made an ungainly progression across the road. Arriving safely at the other side, he set her down on her feet to the cheers and applause of the onlookers. Andrew gave a theatrical bow and offered Jill his arm to take. She, for her part, tried to poke him with a crutch and almost overbalanced. He caught her just in time, to further whoops and yells.

'You need a drink after that,' said one of the men, opening the pub door for them. 'Let me buy you one. That's the funniest thing I've seen today.'

Soon, Jill was settled in front of a blazing fire, and sipping a glass of very acceptable whisky. It warmed its way down her throat and left her feeling relaxed and happy. She was enjoying herself and so was Andrew, by the looks of things. He was propped up at the bar, in deep discussion with a couple of men and sipping whisky. They had ordered their meal, and were only waiting for the summons through to the dining-room.

Jill took another mouthful of the amber coloured spirit, and gazed into the fire. It was really too hot sitting so close, but she didn't want to move. The flames leapt and flickered mesmerically, and her mind drifted. An image of the old drunk man she'd met in the park appeared, and his voice whispered to her again, 'Is he old?'

'About thirty.'

'Guid-looking?'

'Yes, I suppose he is.'

'Married?'

'No.'

'Rich?'

'Well, it's his own business, and it seems to be doing well.'

'So, what's stopping ye?'

'What do you mean?'

'Marry him, hen. He sounds like a guid catch.'

Did she want to marry him? Was she falling in love with him? What were her feelings towards him, her true feelings, not what she thought she ought to be feeling towards him? She looked over to the bar where he stood. He looked so relaxed, so at ease with himself and his companions, so enjoying where he was and what he was doing. This was the Andrew she liked – no, loved; not the stressed-out workaholic who was driven to working all hours and who sought perfection in all he touched. If she was with him all the time, she could help him relax more, they could go away together for breaks, they could enjoy nights in with a nice bottle of Australian wine and soft music playing…

No! Definitely no! Was this what she had studied years for? Spent four years teaching in an isolated community to save money for this trip for? Was she going to throw it all away now? She gave herself a mental shake and tossed back the remains of her drink. She was over in Scotland to see the country, and just as soon as she got rid of the crutches, she intended heading off in Linda's car and touring around. On her own. By herself.

'Dinner's ready.' Andrew was collecting her crutches and tucking them under his arm. 'There's not much room between the tables for you to be swinging these things about, so lean on me and I'll help you to our table.'

As soon as they began to move, one of the men Andrew had been talking to rushed over and slipped his arm under hers. 'Right, Andrew, ready when you are. Lift!'

Between them, they carried Jill into the tiny dining-room, where several tables were squashed together. She was plonked down on a chair beside the window, and the table pushed closer. She couldn't have moved if she'd wanted to.

'Thanks, Jim,' said Andrew, sitting opposite her.

'Enjoy your meal,' said the man, going back to the bar.

She didn't know whether it was the fresh country air or just the delicious smells emanating from the kitchen, but she suddenly found her appetite. They tucked into mouth-watering venison in a port and blueberry sauce – a piece of meat that had been running across the hills around them only the previous week.

Everything was cooked fresh, and the vegetables had been picked from the garden that morning. Even the potatoes were home-grown.

'Who's the gardener?' Jill asked when Bob, the owner and chief cook, came to take away their empty plates.

'Oh, that's Morag my wife. She's the green-fingered one. She grows the fruit and veg, and I think up ways to cook it. It's a good system we have.'

'The food's bursting with flavour,' Andrew said. 'What a difference from shop-bought stuff.'

'Wait till you taste the raspberry crumble,' said Bob. 'We've had an excellent crop this year and we've even made jam, we've had so many. If you come over for breakfast, I'll put some out with your toast.'

'That's a date,' said Andrew. 'Breakfast it is.'

The raspberry crumble lived up to their expectations and, replete after their meal, they lingered over the coffee and mints.

'Glad you came?' asked Andrew.

Jill nodded sleepily. Neither of them had had much sleep last night, after the unexpected trip to the hospital, and full stomachs and warm surroundings were making them both drowsy.

'Come on, Sleeping Beauty,' said Andrew. 'We'd better head home.'

This time, they crossed the road with a great deal more style. Andrew took her crutches first, and opened the door to the cottage. He remembered to duck, and went inside to switch on lights. Then he ran back across and picked Jill up from the chair where she was sitting beside the door, and carried her over the road and into the front room.

Gently, he set her down, holding her steady as she stood with her injured foot raised.

'Thanks,' she murmured, all too aware of his closeness. Aware, too, that he hadn't loosened his grip around her body, that his mouth was moving slowly closer to hers, that she could feel his hot, sweet breath on her face. Jill closed her eyes and let her mouth move upwards towards his.

24

She thought she was in heaven when she woke. It certainly looked like that. The sun was streaming through the window, and leaving glinting splashes on the blue and green quilt. She could smell fresh coffee brewing, and she felt relaxed and, yes, happy. A warm feeling was drifting through her, though she couldn't quite understand why.

It took her a moment to accept that she hadn't dreamt their love-making, that she had indeed shared his bed and his love last night, and that she wanted more than anything to do it all over again. She remembered half-waking in the night to the sound of his heavy, not quite a snore, breathing, and feeling comforted and reassured by it. She had turned over and tucked herself spoon-fashion into his broad back, and quickly gone back to sleep. Until now. She hadn't even heard Andrew getting up.

His now familiar off-key whistling started up from the kitchen, a slightly out of tune version of one of the reels they had danced to at the ball. Was that only a few days ago? It felt like a lifetime. She stretched out her injured foot and tested its flexibility by wriggling her toes and trying to move it from side to side. Still tender and not wanting to have any weight on it, she was sure.

The whistling stopped and then restarted, a slower tune this time, and not one she recognised at first. She listened intently, the tune becoming more familiar as she hummed along to it. Then his clear baritone voice sang the words…

Ae fond kiss, and then we sever;
Ae fareweel, alas, for ever!

She bit her lip. Surely he didn't feel like that about her? Not after the passion of the night?

In the kitchen, Andrew sipped his freshly brewed coffee and listened for signs of life from the bedroom. When she woke, he'd take a cup into her. He couldn't believe how he was feeling now. Where had the determination of only a few days ago gone to? Where were his plans of taking Jill to the ball and then leaving for his break so that, when he returned, she would have left her job and Margery would be reinstalled? Where was the decision that Jill was not suitable as a life partner for him? That she was only passing through, as it were, and would return to Australia when her time was up? That his business still needed his whole undivided attention until it was solidly on its feet? That he wasn't over Nicola, the love of his life up to that point?

None of that mattered now. He was here with Jill for a whole week; a whole week which seemed to stretch into infinity. How on earth could he overturn all those decisions he'd made after long and careful thought? He'd been logical and thorough, thinking through all the pros and cons, using his head and not his heart, and making his mind up only after weighing up everything. But love didn't work like that. You couldn't be logical where love was concerned, otherwise Romeo would never have fallen in love with Juliet, Rochester with Jane Eyre, Darcy with Elizabeth Bennett. And Andrew with Jill. He took another sip of the coffee. Had he made it especially strong? Was that why his heart was racing, skipping beats, thumping in his chest? Or was it something else? Something that was making him stare out of the kitchen window with a silly grin on his face, or whistle songs that reminded him of her?

Ae fond kiss and then we sever...

No, not that one. Robert Burns was parting from his beloved when he wrote that. Andrew thought for a moment and then he sang...

My luv is like a red red rose that's newly sprung in June,
My luv is like a melody that's sweetly played in tune...

Andrew took another sip of his coffee and gazed out of the window. The hills in the distance were covered with a purple haze from the heather in bloom, while closer to the cottage he could see two male pheasants, their long tails sweeping the rough grasses as they searched for food. Overhead, a kestrel hovered, watching its prey before dive-bombing down and, after a brief pause, taking off again. It had caught something, Andrew could see, but it was too far away to make out what it was. The only sounds to be heard were the chattering of thrushes and blackbirds in the bushes at the side of the cottage. The brambles which sprawled along the wall of what passed for the garden were laden with ripening fruit, and the birds were eagerly feeding on them. Andrew saw a robin and a finch, but of which type he couldn't identify.

'It's quite a while since I got my bird-watching badge in the cubs,' he said to himself. 'Next time we come up here, I'll bring a bird book.'

So, there was to be a next time? Another visit to the cottage with Jill? One when she wouldn't be hampered with a damaged ankle, and he could take her hiking over the moors and maybe even climb a Munro – those tempting hills that reached the giddy heights of 3000 feet. He would have to make sure she had the proper equipment; when the weather changed, Arctic winds could make the hills a dangerous place to be.

He was musing over what sort of boot Jill would need, when he heard her stirring. She was awake. Rising, he poured another cup of coffee and then paused. What did she take in it? He couldn't remember. Did she take it black or with milk? Sugar or no sugar? There was so much they had to learn about each other, so much back-story to their lives that each was ignorant of.

He placed the cup on a tray, and added the carton of milk and a sachet of sugar he'd found in a cupboard. As he took a spoon from the cutlery drawer, he wished he had a red rose to add to the tray. Then he remembered the wild roses clambering up the front of the cottage. Quietly, he opened the front door and, remembering to duck, went outside. Most of the roses were past their best, but there was one small pale pink one just opening out. He plucked it from the bush and, going back inside again without bumping his head, he placed it on the tray and carried it into the bedroom.

Jill was sitting up in bed, her loose silk dressing gown wrapped around her. Her eyes lit up when she saw the tray, and she smiled happily at Andrew.

'Good morning, my love,' she said. 'I hope you intend keeping this up every morning.'

'Now, darling, you know I will,' he replied, settling the tray down on her knees and bending to kiss her.

The coffee almost spilt as she responded to his touch, but they drew apart just in time. Jill picked up the rose and sniffed it.

'Agh!' she yelled. 'What's that?'

Creeping out from the petals was a tiny beetle.

'Don't worry,' said Andrew, brushing it onto his hand and carrying it over to the window, 'they're quite harmless, if a bit unexpected. Not quite the romantic gesture I intended.'

He opened the sash window and let it crawl outside.

'If it had been an Australian one, you wouldn't have been treating it quite so casually,' she said. 'Some of our tiny insects pack quite a punch.'

'There's nothing over here that can give you more than a bit of a nibble,' Andrew said, plonking himself down on the bed. 'Apart from midges, that is. They can be infuriating.'

'What are midges?'

'Tiny wee insects that hover round your head in clouds, and bite. They're particularly bad in the late spring and summer, but hopefully by now the worst is past. They don't come out on days when there's a breeze, so let's hope for one.'

'What have you got planned for today?' Jill asked as she sipped her coffee.

'It's a beautiful morning. What say we have breakfast across the road and then head off in the car somewhere? There are lots of beauty spots round here I'd like to show you.'

'Sounds good,' said Jill. 'Especially the breakfast with homemade raspberry jam. But don't you want to go walking in the hills?'

'Without you? No, that can wait till your ankle's better. I thought today we could drive to Aberfoyle, then over the Duke's Pass to Brig o' Turk. You'll be able to have a good look at Loch Achray and Loch Venachar. They're stunning, and on a bright day like this, it should be perfect.'

· · ·

AFTER BREAKFAST, Jill managed to climb into the front seat beside Andrew. By pushing the seat as far back as it could go, she could have more room to rest her foot.

'It's not too long a drive, and we'll have plenty of stops for you to take photos. You did bring your camera with you?'

Jill nodded. It had been one of the things she'd bought before leaving Australia – an essential if she was touring Scotland. Already, she had taken many pictures in and around Edinburgh, and emailed some to Aunt Linda to pass on to her mum. She wasn't quite sure how she was going to explain how she came to be sharing a cottage and a bed – though she definitely wasn't mentioning that – with Andrew, but she'd deal with that later and just gloss over it at present. Which reminded her, she hadn't checked her phone for what seemed like ages.

While Andrew drove, she rummaged in her handbag, opening pockets and searching through its depths, but to no avail.

'I think I must have left my phone in Edinburgh,' she confessed. 'I can't find it anywhere in my bag.'

'What do you need a phone for, when we're in the middle of nowhere?' Andrew smiled. 'The reception probably isn't great around here. But you can always use mine, if you want.'

'I was just going to text my mum and tell her what a great time I'm having, but I'll leave it for the moment.'

She settled back and let the pleasures of the day come to her. The air was mild with brief spells of sunshine when it broke through the high-level haze, and just the hint of a breeze.

'No self-respecting midge will venture out in it. Spoils its hairdo,' claimed Andrew.

It was even warm enough to enjoy a cup of coffee sitting outside at the visitor centre, amongst the tall trees of the forest.

'Pity we're too late to see the ospreys,' said Andrew, reading the information sheet he'd picked up. 'They're beautiful birds.'

Jill was quite happy just to prop her foot up on a spare chair and look about her. There were still quite a few visitors, though the summer rush was over. She saw some of them glance over and knew they were categorising them as a couple. A warm feeling filled her, and she looked across at Andrew, his head bowed over the sheet he was reading, his dark hair flopping over his forehead making him look much more boyish and young than usual.

She liked this Andrew she was seeing. She couldn't reconcile it with the grumpy, moody man that she had witnessed in Edinburgh. He had definitely been in need of a holiday. He worked far too hard for his own good.

'Penny for them.' Andrew was grinning at her.' You were miles away. What were you thinking about?'

'You.'

'Oh dear,' he groaned. 'Any particular failing?'

'I was just thinking how different you are here. Not grumpy or moody, like at the flat.'

He looked away to the horizon where just a glimpse of a loch glittered as the sun hit it.

'Things are different here,' he said in a low voice.

'You were needing a break from your work.'

'I would still have been moody and grumpy if I'd been here without you.'

'Why? What difference do I make?'

His head turned, and his dark brown eyes fixed on her.

'A huge difference, especially after last night.'

'You just wanted to sleep with me?'

'No,' he said vehemently. 'Not just that. Of course I wanted to sleep with you, but do you know how unsettling you are? How you've tormented me all those weeks since you arrived. I didn't plan to fall in love with you, in fact, I did my damnedest not to, but I just couldn't not do it.'

He looked away. Almost shyly, Jill thought. Definitely a Scot; not keen on talking about or showing his emotions. And they were strong emotions. She could see that. She smiled to herself and took his hand.

'And now that you have fallen in love with me, is it as bad as you expected?'

'Don't be silly,' he said, his face lightening. 'You know it's wonderful, isn't it?'

'Yes,' she agreed, and their heads bent together for a quick kiss.

They drew apart, and Andrew finished up the crumbs of his shortbread while Jill suddenly found her mouth opening and herself saying,

'Who's Nicola?'

A darkness came over him. He frowned, and that tic in his jaw pulsed.

'How do you know about her?'

'Linda mentioned how you'd both taken her to the Tattoo. I just wondered who she was.'

There was a pause. Jill mentally kicked herself for her big mouth again, but she kept silent. Maybe it was time to hear from Andrew just what Nicola had meant to him.

'At one time,' he began, 'she was very special to me. Very, very special. We were together for more than two years and I thought we'd get married, but it didn't work out. We started having arguments about silly things, and they'd escalate into blazing rows. I had just started my business, and I suppose I spent too much time on it and not enough on our relationship. So, one day she told me she'd met someone else and that she was leaving me.'

Jill stroked his hand. 'How awful for you,' she said. 'You must have been devastated.'

Andrew nodded. 'I was. I threw myself into my business, to block it all out. I couldn't bear to think about it, so I worked so hard I didn't have any spare time to do so.' His hand moved to encompass hers. 'I'm beginning to learn it wasn't exactly the best way of dealing with it, because it's taken me far longer to get over it than it should. Right until yesterday, in fact.'

'And now?'

'I'm over her for good. It's you I love now. It's you I want to spend time with.'

Their heads bent together for a longer, more passionate kiss, only interrupted by a tut-tutting from a woman carrying a tray with two cups of coffee and ham sandwiches to the table beside them. Andrew and Jill drew apart and grinned at each other, especially when her obviously henpecked husband, trailing behind, winked at them.

The woman noisily clattered the cups and plates down onto the table, and propped the plastic tray by the side of the table leg. It immediately slipped to the floor with a crash.

'Come on,' Andrew whispered, 'let's find somewhere quieter.'

He handed the crutches to Jill, and helped her up. As she was gripping the handles and steadying herself ready for the off, she was pleased to see the woman looking rather contrite. Even better, the couple had to move to let Jill past their table, the tray once more clattering to the floor.

'What a killjoy,' Andrew muttered, as they made their

slow way out to the car. 'Fancy being married to the likes of her.'

'I felt sorry for him,' Jill answered, slowly making her way down the disabled ramp beside the stairs. 'He can't have much of a life.'

25

The rest of the day was spent stopping at every viewpoint and a few other places, as Jill squealed with delight at the scenery round every bend. Her camera had a busy time of it snapping the views, as well as the lone kilted piper standing by the side of the road playing a selection of Scottish airs.

'That's just for the tourists,' Andrew scoffed. 'He's probably a civil servant or a dustman or something, earning an extra bit of cash.'

'I'm a tourist,' said Jill. 'Here, you take a picture of me standing next to him.'

She hobbled over to the piper, who obligingly held out an arm to steady her. Somehow, the arm continued round her waist and, when she looked at him, she was surprised to see how young he was.

'What do you do the rest of the time?' she asked, while Andrew fiddled with the camera settings.

'I've just left school,' he grinned. 'I'm trying to earn a bit of money for when I go to University next month.'

'Smile, please,' said Andrew.

The camera clicked, and the young man released his arm.

'What are you going to study?' Andrew asked.

'Business management and tourism,' the young man answered.

'Well, in four years or whenever you finish, give me a ring,' Andrew said, fishing in his wallet and taking out his business card. 'You've got initiative.'

'What about a summer job next year?'

Andrew burst out laughing. 'Ok, I like your style. Ring me then.'

They got back in the car and, with a cheery wave at the piper who was once more tuning up his pipes, they drove off.

By the time they reached Margery's cottage late in the afternoon, the combination of all that fresh air and the emotions of the last few days got to Jill, and she yawned deeply.

'Lie down for an hour,' counselled Andrew. 'I'll go for a walk up that hill there,' and he nodded out of the window.

When she woke, Jill discovered that she must have slept for well over an hour. The sun was slowly moving down the sky, though it wouldn't completely set for some time yet.

Where was Andrew? Was he back? She listened intently but could hear no noise from the lounge. Had he perhaps gone to the pub for a pint after his walk?

She struggled out of bed and made her way into the lounge. It was just as they had left it, her camera still sitting on the coffee table and her bag lying open beside it. But of Andrew there was no sign.

Jill sat down on a chair beside the window looking onto the hill where he had been heading. A soft breeze riffled through the leaves of the bushes in the garden, and she watched as the blackbirds pecked at the remaining fruits on the brambles. She wished she had a pair of binoculars so that she could train them on the hillside to see if she could spot Andrew. Surely it was the type of thing that Margery would keep in the cottage? Where would she put them? Jill gazed round the room, at the fireplace forlornly full of the previous night's ashes, at the homely armchairs and sofa, at the collection of well-thumbed paperbacks lying higgledy-piggledy on the shelf beside the mantelpiece. Then she remembered the cupboard in the hall with the fishing rods and Wellington boots. That would probably be the place to keep binoculars.

With a struggle, she hobbled through to the hall and opened the cupboard. Old jackets and coats hid the shelves behind, so she had to burrow into them to see what was there. As the shelves got lower and her ankle more tender, she sank down on all fours and crawled deep in among the boots and hiking gear.

She had to feel around for the best part, as the light couldn't penetrate to the back of the cupboard. With the coats muffling all sound, she didn't hear a dull thud followed by several expletives as Andrew once again forgot to duck coming in.

Jill did, however, almost scream with shock when she felt someone pat her lightly on her behind.

Reversing out of the cupboard was a bit of a scramble, but when she did, her hair hanging over her face and a fishing rod hooked into her sweater, Andrew burst out laughing.

'What on earth are you doing?' he said between snorts of laughter. 'No, let me guess. You're looking for the Scottish equivalent of Narnia.'

Jill disentangled the fishing rod and poked him with it.

'Wrong,' she said, tossing it aside. 'Help me up.'

'You're playing hide and seek, and I've found you,' Andrew continued, as he helped her back into the lounge.

'Wrong again. You've only one more guess,' Jill said, making herself comfortable on the sofa and resting her ankle along its length.

'You're looking for a secret underground passage to the pub, so we don't have to go through that performance again tonight and entertain the locals for free.'

'Completely wrong,' said Jill. 'I win.'

'So, what *were* you doing?'

'I was looking for a pair of binoculars so that I could watch for you coming off the hill.'

'You'd never have found them,' said Andrew. 'I took them with me.' He pointed to where he had laid them down on the coffee table. 'And I saw a golden eagle with them. And a couple of stags.'

'So, you had a good walk?'

'Glorious. When your ankle's better, we'll do the walk together. It's not too difficult and at this time of day it's perfect, as the creatures are around, looking for food.'

Jill felt that now familiar warm glow at the mention of the future. Theirs. Together. She watched as Andrew bent down to clear out the fire and set it with rolled-up newspaper and twigs for kindling. The dark hair at the back of his neck curled over the crew neck of his sweater, and she longed to reach out and stroke it. He turned and saw her watching him.

'Why are you looking at me like that? Have I got a hole in the back of my jeans?' he asked.

'No, silly,' she replied, ruffling his hair with her hand. 'I just like looking at you.'

'Good,' he said. 'Just as well I like looking at you, too. We can sit and stare at each other all night.'

'How about across a table laden with food? Come on, let's eat. I'm starving, and you must be too after your walk.'

'Ok. Give me a minute to tidy up and we'll go.'

In the time it took Jill to scramble to her feet and dragoon her crutches into behaving themselves, Andrew was ready.

'I wonder what's on the menu tonight,' he said, heading towards the front door.

'Duck,' said Jill. 'Duck!'

Too late, Andrew's forehead and the door lintel met yet again.

'I did warn you,' she said.

'I thought you were talking about the menu,' was the rueful reply, as he rubbed the sore spot.

Duck wasn't on the menu, but locally-caught trout was. It was delicious, as was the Atholl Brose which followed.

'We had this at that reception for the Ukrainian ballet troupe, remember?' said Jill, tucking into its creamy sweetness.

'How could I forget? That Lutsenko was far too keen on you.'

Jill smiled. 'Yes, he was a bit. He was gorgeous, though.'

'What happened between you?' Andrew's eyes were dark, and a deep cleft appeared between his eyebrows.

'Nothing.' Jill looked straight at him. 'Absolutely nothing. Grigor was great to talk to and he made me feel good, as my confidence wasn't exactly brimming over. But nothing whatever happened. Not even a chaste goodnight kiss.'

Andrew's face regained its composure. 'Phew!' he said. 'Do you know, I had a pretty sleepless night imagining what you could be doing with him?'

'That's ridiculous. I walked home past his hotel and got

back to my flat, probably not much after you. Your light was still on. I could see its glow in the skylight above the door.'

'I know, I heard you. But I still couldn't sleep.'

'So, you were keen on me even then?'

'Ever since I heard your dulcet Australian tones in the car park that day we met. I thought you were simply a breath of fresh air blown in from down-under.'

'Well, I can't say I thought much of you.'

'I know. I'm sorry. Let's go back to the cottage and make up.'

'Be friends again?'

'Just good friends.'

Jill groaned theatrically as he helped her out of her seat.

Back at the cottage, Andrew switched on his phone to check for messages. Jill saw his brow furrow again as he read one.

'Trouble?' she asked.

'Margery wants me to ring her. Says it's urgent.' He dialled the number and waited for her to pick up.

'Margery,' he said at last. He listened, his frown ever deeper.

'She's here with me,' he said. He listened some more, then said, 'Ok, I'll tell her to do it right away.'

'What have I forgotten to do?' said Jill. 'I thought I'd left everything up to date in the office.'

'It's not the office,' said Andrew, coming to sit beside her. 'It's Linda. She's been trying to phone you, but of course, you left your phone in the flat. She phoned Margery.' He reached out and held her hand. 'She wants you to phone home immediately.'

26

T he journey back to Edinburgh in the dark was a
living nightmare to Jill. Andrew drove as fast as he
could while Jill sat beside him, watching the car headlights
sweep over the road, illuminating snatches of trees and
bushes, cottages and fields. They passed through villages
and small towns, but what their names were, Jill couldn't
see or care.

Her mind was solely on the phone call home. Andrew
had immediately passed over his phone to her, and with
trembling fingers she had pressed the keys of her number
in Australia. Linda had answered, and her news had made
Jill's mind up. She had to get home as quickly as she could.
No ifs or buts or maybes; she wanted home and as soon as
possible. Andrew had nodded as she told him what had
happened through her tears, and he at once began packing
and closing up the cottage.

It had been after midnight when they left on the long
drive to Edinburgh, but Jill didn't feel tired. Obviously, the
adrenaline was keeping her going. And Andrew, too.

'I'll get on to my travel agent as soon as they open in

the morning,' he said. 'They're excellent. They'll pull out all the stops to get you home a.s.a.p. As soon as we've got you booked on a flight, you can let Linda know.'

Jill could only be grateful for his help. She wouldn't have known where to start, but Andrew took on everything with a quiet efficiency. And now all she could do was sit back and let him drive her.

They didn't say much on the journey, but Jill's mind kept revolving round what Linda had told her. There was nothing Jill could have done; there was nothing Jill could do, except simply be there. And that was what she intended – as quickly as she could. All thoughts of staying on in Scotland were gone, all her plans to tour had vanished, all her thoughts of a future with Andrew had disappeared in a puff of smoke. Nothing mattered except to get home and see her mum.

It was still dark when they reached their flats, but in an hour or two it would be light. Andrew helped her up the winding stair to Linda's flat, and opened the door for her.

'Can I get anything for you?' he asked.

Jill shook her head.

'Catch some sleep, and I'll waken you as soon as I hear from the travel agent. You need your rest. You've a long journey ahead of you, and a difficult time once you're there.'

All Jill could do was nod dumbly and fall into bed. All she wanted was for him to be beside her and comfort her, but instead he left her and returned to his own flat. Had she lost Andrew, too? Was he going to resort to being the old Andrew now they were back in Edinburgh? After all, his holiday was spoiled. Instead of the fresh air and rest that he had expected, he was now having to find her a flight home and see her off on her lengthy journey back to Australia.

She was sure she wouldn't sleep, her mind too full of what was going on so far away. But suddenly she heard Andrew's voice, and felt him shake her awake. She opened her eyes to the light streaming through the window and the noise and bustle of the street below. Obviously, she had slept for a while, as the day was well on, judging by the traffic sounds.

Just then, a tour bus, its commentary blaring out, paused at the ancient building across the street and regaled its passengers with its long history.

It gave Jill time to pull herself together and shake the sleep from her before Andrew could tell her what he had managed to arrange.

'We'll have to leave in half an hour,' he said at last, when the tour bus moved away. 'Can you manage it?'

Jill nodded and threw the bedclothes aside.

'You leave from Glasgow,' he continued. 'There's a flight this afternoon, which stops in Dubai. You have a wait there for a connecting flight, but you'll be able to get some sleep before your flight direct to Brisbane. I've emailed Linda with all the arrangements, and hopefully she'll meet you at the airport.'

Jill nodded again and limped towards the shower. Pausing, she turned back to him. 'Thanks,' she said. 'Thanks for everything.'

In the shower, she let her tears flow. She was crying for her mum, for herself, and her lost hopes. But mainly for her mum. She'd let the future take care of itself.

She directed Andrew's packing of her case as she sat on the bed and ate the toast he'd made for her. She wasn't hungry but forced it down, aware that she would need all her strength.

'How will I manage through security and customs with

these?' She gesticulated at her crutches propped up beside her.

'I told the travel agent to alert the airline,' Andrew replied. 'Someone will be there to help you. And the seats will be long enough for you to stretch out your leg.'

Within the thirty minutes, she was packed and ready to go. Andrew loaded her luggage into the car first, before returning up the stairs to help her down. She remembered the first day that she'd flip-flopped down these stairs en route to the car park and her first meeting with him. It felt an age away, so much had happened between them. And now it was almost over. She didn't know when, if ever, she would be able to return to Scotland, would climb these winding stairs, would see Andrew again.

By the time she reached the car, her tears were flowing again.

Andrew held her and kissed her wet cheeks. 'Everything will turn out fine,' he said. 'Be positive. Your mum doesn't want to see you like this.'

Then he helped her into the car.

The journey to Glasgow Airport took longer than expected. The traffic had built up because of road works, and in parts the motorway was reduced to a crawl. Jill could see the tic in Andrew's jaw pulsing strongly, and knew he was worried they wouldn't make the flight in time. Silently, she prayed for the traffic to ease and for a straight run to the airport.

At last, they were streaking through the city centre section and over the Kingston Bridge.

'Not long now,' Andrew said, relief bringing his shoulders down and a smile to his face. 'Don't worry, you'll make it.'

And they did. He was signalled into a parking bay close

to the terminal building, where a uniformed man was waiting with a wheelchair.

'I'm not going in that,' Jill protested, as Andrew helped her out of the car.

'If you want to catch the flight, you are. They're not going to wait while you hobble slowly across the concourse. Anyway, it's a long walk to the gate, and an even longer one to the plane.'

Her ticket was waiting for her at the flight desk, and she quickly checked in her luggage, surprised to find that a girl in the corporate uniform of the airline had been delegated to see her safely on to the plane.

'You've certainly seen to everything,' she said to Andrew, as she was wheeled to the security check. How banal, she thought, to be talking of such minor matters when I'm about to leave him forever.

The girl paused at the entrance to the security area. 'I'm afraid you'll have to make your farewells now,' she said. 'Only passengers beyond this point.'

Andrew's and Jill's eyes met. He bent towards her and kissed her softly on the lips.

'Take care,' he said, his voice husking with emotion. 'Look after yourself. And your mum.'

'Thanks,' Jill said, her throat closing. Her eyes were suddenly full of tears, and she turned to wipe them quickly away. The girl pushed the chair into security, Jill craning her head back to glimpse Andrew, his hand raised in a final farewell.

She had little time to contemplate their low-key parting. Were all final goodbyes like that? She was quickly checked through security, the girl pushing her to the front of the queue, people giving way to the wheelchair. The girl, whose name badge said Tara, wheeled her into a quiet lounge, parked her beside the window overlooking the runway, and brought her a coffee and some biscuits.

'We'll be boarding shortly,' she told Jill. 'I'll come and get you then.'

And indeed, Jill had only finished her coffee and sent a brief text to Andrew to say thank you again and send her love, when Tara returned and they set off to the gate. Again, Tara marched her up to the head of the queue, and Jill was wheeled on ahead of the other passengers. Just as she was about to board, Andrew texted her.

Missing you already. Love you lots.

A lump came to Jill's throat as she read it. She bit back more tears, and slipped her phone in her bag as they reached the aircraft door.

'You'll be fine now,' said Tara, as a steward from the flight came forward to help her out of the wheelchair. 'Hal will take care of you.'

It wasn't till she was settled in her seat, her crutches stowed in a locker, and looked about her, that she spotted Andrew had booked her into business class. No wonder she had so much room to stretch out her legs and ease her sore one into a comfortable position. He'd thought of everything. Quickly, she sent another text to him.

IOU big time. I'll pay my debts when I come back.

She didn't know if she ever would, but she was determined to put a positive spin on things. As Linda had said on the phone, worrying never helps when you don't know what's ahead of you.

Once they were in the air, Jill settled back with a glass of whisky in her hand. It wasn't the time for a drink, but she felt that she needed one to calm her and to help her sleep. Instead, her mind went back to Linda's news. Her mum had found a lump in her breast, she'd been to the specialist, and now they were going to remove it as they were pretty sure it was malignant. She would be having the operation the day after tomorrow. No, she corrected herself, tomorrow. In Australia, it already was tomorrow.

Her pulse quickened. Would she be back in time to see her mum before the operation? Rummaging in her bag, she brought out her ticket information. Yes, she would arrive in Brisbane in the early morning, Thursday it would be then. If she could get a cab right away, and if Mum wasn't scheduled for an early appointment in the theatre, then she might just manage to see her.

As ANDREW STOOD WATCHING Jill being wheeled away out of his life, he felt so bereft, as if the life had been drained from him. He gripped the hand rail and stood for a moment, other hand raised in a farewell salute as Jill disappeared into the security area. She was gone. Would he ever see her again? Would she ever come back to Edinburgh? Was this another heart-breaking time when nothing would ease the pain? Quickly, he texted his love to her, his words winging to her as she waited for take-off.

Andrew headed to the nearest cafeteria and took a coffee to sit at the window looking on to the runway. When at last he saw the flight thunder down the runway and lift up into the air, he knew that Jill was really gone from his life. Gritting his teeth to stop his feelings showing, he headed out of the terminal and back to his car.

Gunning it as hard as he could, he drove out of the city and headed north, back to the cottage. At least there, he would have peace to grieve his loss and to remember the good times they'd had together. At least there, her perfume might still be fresh and the bed still sunken to the shape of their two bodies. At least there, he could remember.

27

Never had Jill felt time pass so slowly. She couldn't concentrate enough on the magazines that were freely available or enjoy the beautifully served food, so different from the usual plastic trays of reheated stodge that she'd had on the flight over. She must have slept, as she woke to find them beginning their descent to Dubai. Again, Andrew had thought of everything. A wheelchair and car waited to take her to a hotel for a shower and a few hours' rest before connecting to the Brisbane flight.

Andrew had texted again

Come back soon when all is well. The cottage awaits.

Yes, she would always remember those few days she'd spent with him. She'd think about the laughs they'd had – him bumping his head on the lintel; her crawling about looking for binoculars; their attempt at crossing the road – these would be the memories she'd treasure. She'd store them away, and when things were bad and she was down in the dumps, then she'd take them out and relive them, and maybe they'd bring a smile back to her cheeks. And when she felt lonely and on her own, there were other memories they'd shared that she would linger over. That night with him when the world disappeared and they were alone in their love for each other, when nothing mattered except the touch of his skin on hers and the caress of his lips on her body. These were her special memories that she'd keep to herself and share with no-one.

My luv is like a red, red rose…

At last, at long last, the flight was almost over. The plane began its descent into Brisbane Airport, and out of the window she glimpsed the Australian coast. There was the deep blue sea with lighter patches where the reef grew up towards the light, the green hinterland, verdant with the early spring rains, and finally, the urban sprawl that was the capital city of Queensland.

Again, staff were on hand to help her off the plane, and a sturdy young employee whisked her in a wheelchair to customs, to baggage, and finally to the arrivals lounge.

'Goodness me,' said a voice with a distinctly Edinburgh accent, and one which Jill immediately recognised. 'What have you done to yourself?'

'Oh Linda,' cried Jill, the tears running down her cheeks. 'It's so good to see you. Tell me what's happening.'

'More importantly, what's happened to you?' Linda eyed the young man still clutching the handles of the chair. 'Can you wheel her out to my car?' she asked.

'No worries. Just lead the way.'

Once Jill was settled in the car and the crutches and luggage stowed in the boot, Linda negotiated her way somewhat erratically through the early morning rush hour traffic and onto the freeway. It was only then that Jill felt able to ask about her mum.

'How is she? When's the operation? Will I be able to see her beforehand?'

'Fine, in an hour, and yes, if I drive like a banshee and hope there are no police about.'

Fortunately, there weren't, and Linda swept into the hospital car park and came to a halt as close to the main entrance as she could manage. She ignored the small fact that the space said Reserved, pointing out to Jill in mitigation that they were an emergency and it was important for Patricia to see Jill before her operation.

'It will cheer her up, and boost her immune system, and help her cope with it all and heal better,' she assured Jill as she commandeered a wheelchair, plonked her niece in it, and proceeded at a lively pace along the corridor to the ward.

Jill clutched onto her crutches with one hand and the arm-rest with the other, as Linda pushed in the same way as she drove, expecting everyone to get out of her way and let her through. Jill was relieved when they reached the ward safely.

Her mum was lying resting on a bed when they arrived, but when she saw Jill in a wheelchair and holding crutches, she immediately sat up in disbelief.

'My poor darling, what have you done to yourself?' she exclaimed in a slightly slurred voice, the sedation having kicked in.

'Nothing much,' replied Jill, reaching over to give her mum a hug and a kiss. 'I pulled some ligaments and I just have to rest my leg till it heals. But never mind about me, how about you?'

'I'm fine,' said Mum. 'Though I wish they'd hurry up. I was supposed to be taken first thing this morning, but there must have been an emergency as I'm still here.'

'Just as well,' said Linda. 'We'd never have made it.'

Patricia took Jill's hand as she sank back into the pillows. 'The stuff they give you beforehand is great,' she mumbled. 'I'm not worried about a thing. I… oh, here comes trouble.'

A smiling nurse appeared at the foot of the bed. 'We're ready for you now, Patricia,' she said. 'Let's get you down to theatre.'

It was quite a procession to the operating theatre. First, Mum sailed along in her bed, pushed by a bronzed young man and accompanied by the nurse, then Jill in her wheelchair, with Linda keeping close behind. But at a set of double doors, they halted.

'This is where you say goodbye to your mum for a couple of hours,' the nurse said to Jill. She stood up and hobbled over to the bed.

'Take care, Mum,' she whispered, her face buried in the neck of her mum's hospital gown. 'I love you.'

Then they were gone, and Jill and Linda were left alone in the corridor.

'She'll be fine,' Linda said, putting her arms around Jill. 'Let's go for a coffee and you can tell me all about your time in Scotland while we wait.'

Jill's mind frantically flicked through her memories as she was wheeled into the lift and down to the cafeteria. What could she tell Linda that wouldn't reveal too much of what had passed between Andrew and herself? Where could she say she'd been? She'd just decided to talk about the events she'd been involved in and the people she'd met at them, when Linda placed an espresso in front of her and said, 'So how did you and Andrew get on? Did you like him?'

To her chagrin, Jill burst into tears again.

'Goodness, I didn't mean to upset you,' Linda said, fishing in her handbag for a spare tissue. 'Here, dry your eyes and tell me all about it.'

'I'm sorry,' Jill said. 'It's a combination of jet lag and

worry over Mum. I'm feeling a bit emotional just now.' She wiped her eyes and took several deep breaths. She wasn't ready to spill the beans quite at the moment.

Linda looked at her for a long minute.

'Ok,' she began. 'How about telling me about the Caledonian Ball? Or the Tattoo?' she added quickly, seeing Jill's lower lip beginning to tremble again.

Jill shook her head and blew her nose, in an attempt to gain control over her feelings.

'All off limits?' Linda said. 'Well, in that case, I'll tell you what I've been doing while I've been in Australia.'

And she did. Jill was grateful for her aunt's loquaciousness as she described where she'd been, who she'd met, and the adventures she'd had with various Australian fauna, including nearly colliding with a large kangaroo on a back road, photographing crocodiles sunning themselves on the banks of a northern river, and holding a carpet python in an animal sanctuary.

By the time she'd finished her travelogue, it was time to return upstairs to see if Jill's mum was out of the operating theatre.

'She shouldn't be long now,' one of the nurses told them, as she bustled along the corridor to another patient. 'We're expecting her back at any time.'

Sure enough, a trolley arrived shortly after, with Patricia still fast asleep. She was wheeled into a bay, and a couple of nurses checked her over and made her comfortable in her bed.

'She's fine, if a bit groggy still,' said one. 'Sit and hold her hand until she wakes. She'll know you're there.'

As LINDA and Jill sat one on either side of her, watching her every breath and wondering privately what the future held, ten thousand miles away in a cottage in Scotland, Andrew paced the floor unable to sleep. The place was filled with Jill and his memories of her, and instead of comforting him as he'd hoped, they only served to aggravate the wound her departure had left. What was he going to do? He couldn't go on feeling like this all over again. He had felt awful when he and Nicola had broken up, but this was ten, no, a thousand times worse.

His mind searched through all the possible ways of dealing with it as he continued to pace up and down the tiny living-room. How on earth could they manage to conduct a long-distance relationship, when neither knew if they would ever be together again? Jill was too worried about her mother to be bothered with him. He would be pushed to the back of her list of important things in her life, and probably fall off the radar before long. And there were all these handsome, tanned Aussie men for her to dally with, if she felt like it. He'd been a fool to let his feelings overwhelm him. He should have listened to his head and not his heart. If he had, he wouldn't be in this state now. He would be enjoying his break and planning tomorrow's hike into the hills, instead of crucifying himself with thoughts of what might have been.

Andrew stopped and stared at the darkness out of the window. He knew the hills were out there, but at the moment, it was totally black; not even a wisp of moonlight illuminating the scene. It fitted exactly how he felt. How on earth was he going to cope with his emotions? He was in love with her, but it wasn't to be. There were too many obstacles in their way. Once again, he would have to throw himself into his work and dedicate himself into building it up into the most successful company in the city, no, the country. It was the only thing that worked. It had to work, and it had to start now.

First thing in the morning, he would head back to the office and get things moving. He had plans for expansion which he would put into operation. And woe betide Dorothy and Margery if they mentioned her name in his hearing.

He went to bed in the room that they had shared and pretended he didn't care about her, until at last, in the early hours, he fell asleep, exhausted.

28

J ill awoke in her own bed at home, and listened to the
sound of a kookaburra raucously welcoming the day.
The sun filtered in through the louvered slats of the
window blind and danced on the thin coverlet on her bed.
It reminded her of the way the sun had glinted on the
blue and green quilt on the bed of the cottage, that
morning after their love-making. For a moment, she
allowed herself the luxury of revisiting her memories.
Then throwing aside the bed-clothes, she manoeuvred
herself out of bed, grabbed her crutches, and headed into
the bathroom. The chooks would need fed – though Linda
had assured her that she was now a competent chicken-
feeder and egg collector – the breakfast made, and things
collected to take into the hospital when they visited her
mother.

Patricia had woken shortly after being brought back to
the ward, and the nurses had assured Jill that she was
doing well and would simply doze for the rest of the day
while the painkillers worked their magic. Jill and Linda had
driven the 60 miles home and had a quick meal before jet

lag and mental exhaustion overtook Jill, and she collapsed into bed.

Now, she was feeling like her old self, and if it wasn't for the impediment of her damaged leg and the necessary crutches, would be more than prepared to do a full day's work. As it was, everything took twice as long and some things were well-nigh impossible, as she discovered when she went out to the henhouse and attempted to gather the eggs. Wielding a basket and crutches at the same time as rummaging around in the nesting boxes was a no-no.

'You're mad, so you are,' said Linda, who had come running out when she saw what Jill was up to. 'Give me that basket and you go back to the house and sit on your bottom for once.'

Jill waved a crutch menacingly at her aunt. 'Just you wait,' she said, mock-threateningly, 'when I get back to normal, I'll make sure you sit there like a lady.'

'Heaven forbid,' said Linda, placing a large white egg in the basket. 'That's the last thing I want to be. Who'd be a lady? How boring! That Nicola fancied herself one. I said to Andrew, after they broke up, that she wasn't his type. You're much more suitable. Oh sorry…' she tailed off as Jill turned and headed back to the house.

Blast her, thought Jill, as she opened the bug screen door. She keeps bringing him up. Why can't she stop talking about him? Can't she see it hurts me? Of course, she could, it was just, well, that was Linda for you. Jill understood where she got her own foot-in-mouth propensity from. Linda had it in spades, too.

She sat down in the kitchen as Linda had suggested, and picked up her phone to text Andrew.

Mum doing fine, she wrote. *Love Jill xxx*

She pressed send, and it disappeared out into the ether. I wonder what he's doing now, she thought. She calculated the time difference – ten hours behind them, so that made it eleven o'clock at night; Thursday night. Jill hesitated. Should she phone? What would he be doing? Was he at his flat, or had he gone to the cottage for the last few days of his holiday? She hesitated, and the moment was lost. Linda came in carrying the egg basket which she set down on the worktop.

'Sorry if I said the wrong thing then,' she said. 'I didn't suspect how bad you were feeling about him. Did you have a fight?'

Jill shook her head, as she couldn't speak for threatening tears again. 'Please don't mention him,' she choked. 'I just don't want to talk about it at the moment. And no,' she continued when she saw Linda's stricken expression, 'we didn't have a fight. We're… we're so far away now, it has to be over.'

'Don't be silly,' said Linda. 'Distance is no object these days. What about email and your phone?' She pointed at Jill's mobile, which she was still clutching.

Jill looked down at it. 'I sent a text,' she whispered.

'Phone him,' ordered Linda. 'He'll want to hear your voice. A text isn't the same.'

'He might have gone to bed.'

'Wake him up. For goodness sake, Jill, where's your gumption? You'll never get anywhere with him if you just sit and stare at the phone. He'll be delighted to talk to you, regardless of the time.'

Linda headed out of the screen door again. 'I'm leaving you to it,' she said, 'and when I come back I expect to see you with a silly grin on your face. It's not going to help Patricia if you go round looking like a wet Monday morning.'

But there was no sound of Andrew's voice answering

her call. Instead, an impersonal female blandly told her to leave a message after the tone.

'Hi, it's Jill,' she began. What on earth could she say? 'I sent a text. Mum's doing fine. We're going to see her again later today. Miss you. Bye.'

That was pathetic, she told herself. Not how she'd thought it would be. She'd hoped he would answer and they could chat. Instead, she'd left a silly little message which conveyed nothing of how she was feeling. She could only hope that he'd ring her himself and they could laugh over it.

But he didn't. Not a call or a text that day, or the next. Not that the phone didn't ring; on the contrary, it rang constantly as a steady stream of friends phoned to find out how her mum was. Every time she heard its jolly jingle, Jill jumped with anticipation, which was quickly dissipated when she saw who the caller was. She spoke to friends from University, neighbours, and far-flung relations, school friends, and people that her mother knew and Jill didn't. But from Andrew there was silence.

Perhaps he was out on the hills, out of range of a signal. Perhaps his phone needed recharging, or he'd lost it, or it had fallen into one of the many little streams – burns – dribbling down the hillsides. Perhaps he simply didn't want to speak to her. As the days went on, that solution appeared to be the most obvious. She'd sent a couple more texts, carefully checking she had the correct number, and letting him know that her mum was doing really well and that she would be starting more treatment shortly. Nothing. Not a text, not an acknowledgement that Andrew had received word from her.

And then one day, about a week after her return, his phone gave out a different signal – a number unobtainable.

Jill sank into a depression. She tried to put on a cheery

face when she and Linda visited the hospital, but at home, she found it hard to maintain her composure and go about her duties as if all was well.

Eventually, her mother was allowed to leave the hospital and continue her treatment at the local one. She was still very tired, and Jill and Linda shared out her care between them, Jill helping as much as her ankle would allow. She had been delighted that her mother was well enough to be at home, but keeping up a cheery side all day long meant that she was relieved to be able to head for bed each evening. She kept up the pretence of tiredness and having to rest her ankle as long as she could, but her mother wasn't deceived.

'You must miss Edinburgh a lot,' she commented, as Jill was painting her nails for her.

Jill kept her head lowered and simply nodded, pretending to concentrate hard on her task.

'And your job,' her mother went on. 'Will it still be there for you when you go back?'

'No,' Jill eventually replied, 'it was only temporary. Anyway,' she tried to inject a teasing note into her voice, 'don't tell me you want rid of me already?'

'Of course not, dear, but… but I feel you should go while Linda's here. It's too good an opportunity to miss.'

'I'll see,' Jill said. 'Now, doesn't that look better? Your nails were rubbish after all that scrubbing about in the garden and yard.'

The moment passed. Patricia held out her hands to admire her manicure while Jill made her a cup of coffee. Linda came in with news from the local town where she'd been shopping, and the conversation moved to the on-goings of the small community.

One day, about four weeks after her fall, Jill made an appointment at her local doctor's surgery and Linda dropped her off while she went for a few shopping items. Jill limped into the waiting room, her crutches now almost not needed unless she was walking for a while, and waited for her name to be called.

'Good day, Jill,' said the doctor, when he opened the surgery door. 'How's it going? Heard you'd done some damage to yourself.'

Jill stared at him, amazed that the last time she'd seen Bradley Johnston had been at the school's prom, before they all went their separate ways. He'd been the High School Hunk of his day, and looked just the same, if a bit more mature and filled out.

'Brad!' she said. 'You're never the doctor here, are you?'

'Part of my training. Six months here and then on to Toowoomba for another stint. So, what happened to you?'

'I fell and hurt my ankle. The hospital said I'd torn some ligaments, strapped it up, and gave me these.' She waved the crutches at him.

'Where did you fall?'

'In the street. It was cobbled and slippy. In Edinburgh,' she continued, seeing the puzzled expression on his face as he tried to think of any Australian cobbles.

'Ah yes, you're the far-flung traveller. So, what are you doing back here?'

'Mum's receiving treatment for cancer, so I came home as quickly as I could.'

'So I heard. Who's her consultant?'

Jill told him the name, and he nodded sagely. 'Best one there is,' he said. 'She'll get the most up-to-date treatment from him. He's very good.'

Jill took comfort from his words as she slipped off her shoe and presented her ankle for his inspection. Gently, he felt around, and then pronounced it well on the way to healing. 'So, you can ditch the crutches any time you like.'

Jill gave a smile of relief. 'What will I do with them?'

'Take them back with you when you go. I'm sure the hospital will need them for someone else. You are going back, aren't you?'

'I-I don't know, it depends on how Mum does.'

'She'll be right as rain in no time. She won't want you hanging around, will she?'

'Probably not, but I'll wait till her treatment's finished. There's no rush. Maybe I'll wait till it's spring there. I don't fancy their winters much.' Jill was aware that she was babbling, but she didn't want him to probe any more deeply. As it was, there was a wisdom in his eyes that she couldn't miss.

'Look here, why don't you join us next week? You look as if you could do with a night out. A crowd of us are going for a barbecue on the beach. You'll know most of them.' He named several old school friends, and Jill found herself agreeing to come.

After all, she couldn't spend all the time waiting for the phone call that was never going to come now.

29

Linda had kept her mouth shut and stopped mentioning Andrew's name to Jill, but she watched and despaired as her niece suffered. Though she was nicely tanned from the Queensland sun again, the girl's face had a gauntness that wasn't there when she'd arrived, her figure was losing its healthy roundness, and all she wanted to do was sit around watching soaps with unseeing eyes.

Eventually, after another week had gone past, Linda could stand it no longer. She headed down to the local Internet cafe, bought herself a large latte, and fired off a strongly worded email which began,

You thoughtless piece of manhood. I know what you're up to, and I'm not letting you behave like that towards my niece. It may have worked when you broke up with Nicola, but it's not going to work again.

It took her nearly twenty minutes of sustained typing before she finished venting her feelings and her spleen, then she read it over, correcting several spelling mistakes she'd made in her haste to say what she felt, and pressed send.

· · ·

A DARK FLUSH spread over Andrew's face as he read the email. A flood of conflicting emotions rushed through him. How dare she interfere in his life like that! What was it to her if he didn't want to see Jill again? But he did, said a persistent voice from deep inside him. He was missing her so much it was like a physical pain. He couldn't sleep, he wasn't eating, and he was tetchy and grumpy at work. Margery and Dorothy went tiptoeing round the office like a couple of scared mice, desperately trying to keep out of his way for fear of aggravating his temper. He was a nightmare to work with, and he was ashamed of himself.

But what could he do? Jill was ten thousand miles away and not likely to return for ages, if at all. He had received her texts and heard her speak on his voicemail; so poignant that he had to brush away the tears before deliberately deleting her message. He couldn't put himself through that all again. Not all that pain, that suffering, when his life took on a grey tinge, and colours and pleasures faded. He just wasn't strong enough to cope. All he could do was to throw himself into his work, and hope that eventually the feelings of despair and dejection and sheer misery would pass.

Linda Naismith was furious with him, her email made that abundantly clear. But Jill was safe at home with her mother, and surely that was where she wanted to be. She had been in Scotland for a working holiday before she had planned to return eventually to Australia. Her mother's illness had only hastened that. She was where she wanted to be, and that wasn't with him in Edinburgh. Wasn't she happy then? Was that why Linda had emailed him? Was Jill as miserable as he was?

A small tickle of hope wormed its way up his spine. Was he wrong, as Linda had vehemently suggested, to behave the way he was? He hadn't thought of Jill's feelings. He was unbelievably selfish, assuming that she didn't care about him, when Linda was telling him otherwise.

He swung his chair round from the computer and rose to pace the floor of his flat. Everywhere he went was filled with her presence; here, in the flat and across the landing in Linda's, Jill had touched his being. Here, they'd partied and argued and had their first kiss; here, they'd begun to change their misconceptions of each other; here, he'd discovered he was falling in love with her, and done his damnedest to stop himself. He picked up the tartan rug that he'd covered her with when she fell asleep on the couch after the party, and held it to his face, vainly trying to find a trace of her scent among its folds.

Was it too late to begin to sort things out with Jill? Could he still salvage their relationship? He could see now how his behaviour must have caused her pain when he didn't reply to her messages. He had been too wrapped up in himself.

The carpet received a considerable amount of wear and tear as he paced a route between lounge and hall to bedroom and back to hall again. His mind whirled as he thought and thought and desperately tried to make sense of himself and his feelings. At last, as dawn was beginning to show its face over the grey Edinburgh tenements, he sat down at the computer and pressed reply.

30

J ill had to admit that it had been nice to meet up with old friends again at the beach barbecue. She had fielded questions about her trip to the UK as quickly and as deftly as she could, and changed the topic of conversation round to the careers and family life of her school friends. One or two were already married and pregnant, or with a young baby, while others were fancy-free and foot-loose, itching to see the world beyond Australasia, and envious of her recent trip. They were also sympathetic about its curtailment, but convinced – to a man (and woman) – that she should return and take up where she left off.

Jill had smiled and laughed and agreed with them, adding the proviso that she was waiting till her mum had the all-clear. Of Andrew, she said nothing. Not even to Judy, who had been her best friend all through primary and high school, only parting to go to different universities: Judy in New South Wales, while Jill had remained in Queensland.

'We must do this again soon,' Brad shouted to everyone, as they were clearing up. 'Anyone got an excuse for a party?'

'Do we need one?' said another guy, collecting the empties that were scattered around.

'Jill,' said Judy, 'it's your birthday in November, isn't it? The 15th? We must celebrate that.'

'Great idea,' said Brad. 'Jill's place, November 15th, for another bash. Everyone up for it?'

A general shout of agreement went up.

'I-I'm not sure if Mum will…' stuttered Jill.

'No worries,' said Judy. 'We'll do the organising. Your place is big enough for us to be far away from the house so that the music won't annoy her.'

'She'll be joining in, if I know your mum,' added Brad. 'And as for that aunt of yours, she's a real party animal, fair dinkum.'

'Yeah,' said Judy. 'That was some party they had for Linda's birthday. It went on until breakfast, and then we cooked eggs and bacon on the barbie. I think just about all of the town was there.'

Jill was bemused to hear what Linda and her mum had been up to while she had been away. They had never had parties like that when Jill was at home. She put it down to her aunt's influence, remembering what people in the Edinburgh close had said about Linda's parties.

When she broached the idea of her birthday party, both Linda and her mum were delighted with the idea and went into a huddle to plan it.

'There are loads of tables and chairs down in the sleep-out,' Patricia said.

'In the what?' asked Linda.

'The sleep-out,' Jill explained. 'That hut near the bottom of the paddock. It's where the worker used to live, when this property had one. Now, we just use it to store things in.'

'I live and learn,' commented Linda. 'It's not just the Americans and us who are divided by a common language.'

For the next few days, any time Jill came into a room, the conversation would stop, and they would smile at her and ask some innocuous question. She knew what they were up to, especially when there were some strange phone calls that hung up when Jill answered, but necessitated Linda or her mum disappearing into another room with the phone if they managed to pick it up first.

Jill convinced herself that she didn't mind all the fuss about what, after all, was only an ordinary birthday, and went along with it – especially when she saw how the colour returned to her mother's cheeks and her energy levels came back, along with her zest for life. It obviously meant a lot to Mum to arrange it all for her, so Jill determined to show her appreciation of all the effort, and to try and enjoy it as much as she could.

But there was a weight around her heart that, no matter how hard she tried, wouldn't go away. She missed Andrew terribly, and wished he was with her to give her a hug when she needed one, to laugh with her and talk to her about life in Edinburgh, to take her out and about, and to make her feel alive again.

Her birthday was only a couple of days away, when Judy insisted that Jill come with her to Brisbane to choose a new outfit for the party.

'What were you actually planning to wear?' she asked. 'Surely not one of your usual outfits?'

'What's wrong with them?' Jill protested. 'I've got loads of pairs of shorts and tops that would do ok, and if you want something posher, what about my long beach dress with the halter-neck?'

'That's quite old,' added her mum. 'You've worn it several times, haven't you?'

'Yes, but it's nice, isn't it? There's nothing wrong with wearing the same thing again, is there?' said Jill.

'But this is your birthday,' Linda said. 'You've got to have something new for your birthday bash.'

They were sitting on the veranda on the familiar cane chairs which, after many years of use, fitted around their bodies and sagged where necessary. It was evening, and the hot sun had at last set after what had been a very humid day. Crickets and frogs chirruped and croaked, and moths battered themselves against the outside lights. Jill sipped an iced beer and felt the cool liquid slide down her throat.

'I want to save my money for another trip some time,' she said. 'I don't need to buy anything, and certainly not to go all the way to Brisbane to do so.'

'It's my birthday present to you,' said Linda.

'And I'll drive you there and buy you lunch,' put in Judy. 'There, that's all settled. I'll pick you up at seven thirty. That way, we can drive when it's cool, and hit the shops when they've opened and it's quiet. We can spend a pleasant morning in their air-conditioned splendour, have a leisurely lunch, a stroll around the city, and be back here by supper.'

'That sounds like a perfect day,' said her mum. 'Go and enjoy yourself. Me and Linda will have a girly day to ourselves, so don't hurry back.'

Jill saw Patricia meet Linda's eye, and they both grinned.

AT JUST AFTER seven thirty the next morning, Linda and

Patricia stood on the veranda, waving as Judy's car drove off with Jill.

'Good,' said Linda, as the car disappeared down the road. 'That's them gone. Now we can get on with things.'

'Are you sure this is what she wants?'

Linda nodded. 'Jill's going to have the best birthday ever.'

31

The morning of her birthday, Jill awoke very early. She lay for a moment listening to the little sounds of an awakening day; the creak of the shingles, a faraway shriek of galahs, a patter of tiny feet as some night creature hastened away to its burrow. Twenty-eight – was that old? She certainly felt years older than she had been on her last birthday. Then, she had been full of hope for the future, full of excitement and curiosity, energy and exuberance at what life might bring. Now, she was only too aware of the frailty of life and how close to death they walked; now, she was aware of the fickleness of love, and of how easily it could be extinguished. Now, she felt mature, a woman, grown-up at last and, she had to admit, more than capable of dealing with all that life could throw at her. She had come through the fire and, like steel, had been tempered by it.

Jill tossed aside her bedclothes, slipped on her t-shirt and jeans, and silently opened the veranda door. The air was prickly cool at present, and sent goosebumps up her arms. But it wouldn't be long before the scorching heat of the sun would blast down on them. Down by the stringy bark gums, tables were already set out, and benches and a selection of chairs – obviously purloined from her friends' houses – were scattered about. The permanent brick barbecue was supplemented by a couple of large bottled gas versions, and they were strategically placed under the largest gums to provide the maximum shade for the cooks.

She moved quietly down the steps in her flip-flops, and walked towards the scene of her forthcoming party bash, keeping her eyes skinned for any snakes. Walking around the paddock in her flip-flops was not recommended, but she surmised that any self-respecting serpent would still be tucked up in its hole, and not be venturing out till the sun was up and it could warm itself in its rays.

She wandered among the chairs, setting one upright and brushing stray gum leaves from one or two others. Maybe they could use the leaves in billy tea – the water heated up over a fire in a billy can, and then a spoonful of tea dropped in with a couple of gum leaves for flavour. Brad was good at swinging the billy can and its contents around his head without spilling a drop, which he claimed improved the flavour considerably.

Jill glanced over at the worker's sleep-out, surprised to see a window open a crack. Linda or Mum must have been in there, rooting about for chairs and tables, and opened a window to let some air in. They've forgotten to close it, she said to herself, and changed direction towards it.

The cool air felt refreshing, and her spirits lifted as she walked. Maybe this would be the beginning of a good year; a year to enjoy, with those dear to her well and happy.

Above her, a kookaburra laughed, and she looked up to see it perched not far above her head.

'You're very noisy,' she told it. 'Couldn't you sing something sweeter?'

As if on cue, the clear note of a bellbird rang out, pure in tone and carrying across the land. Alongside it, a whistling – a low, slightly off-key whistle, more tuneful than the bird, and very human. Jill stood stock-still, the hair on the back of her neck quivering. Then softly, she heard a voice sing. The tune was all too familiar, and the words she knew.

My luv is like a red, red rose
That's newly sprung in June...

Galvanised, she sprinted towards the sleep-out and shoved open the door.

Andrew stood there with his arms open. Jill ran into them, and felt his strong, lithe body enfold her.

His lips searched for hers, and they kissed long and deeply. When they moved apart, Jill ran her hands over his face in astonishment.

'What are you doing here? When did you arrive? Did you know it was my birthday?' she burst out.

'Hold on,' said Andrew, 'one question at a time. I've come for your party, and I arrived yesterday, and I'm utterly jet lagged, which is why I'm up and about at this time.'

They kissed again, while outside, the kookaburra laughed its delight.

'Why are you in here and not up at the house?' Jill asked, as she eventually dragged herself away from his lips.

'I'm a surprise for you,' Andrew replied, kissing the golden skin beneath her ear. She didn't bother replying, too engrossed in the feelings flooding over her as his kisses worked their way down her body.

Andrew drew her over to the camp bed where he'd spent the night, and together they lay down and entwined their bodies in the narrow space.

'I love you, Jill,' he whispered, as he held her close.

'I love you, too,' came the soft reply.

THE MORNING SUN had risen quite high in the sky by the time Andrew and Jill emerged from the sleep-out.

'I hope they've left us some breakfast,' Jill said, as they walked hand-in-hand to the house.

'So that's what you think of my love-making?' Andrew grinned. 'Something that gives you an appetite?'

'An appetite for you, darling,' she said, smiling up at him.

They stopped to kiss again.

'OH LORD,' said Linda, glancing out the window. 'She's found him.'

'Whatever made her think of going to the sleep-out?' answered Patricia, joining her at the window. 'She never usually goes there.'

'Well, she's found her birthday surprise, and she seems to be enjoying it,' said Linda.

'Better put fresh coffee on.' Jill's mum bustled about in the kitchen, laying out cups and plates, while Linda watched the happy couple's dilly-dallying progress towards the house.

As they climbed the veranda steps together, Linda opened the screen door.

'Welcome to the house, Andrew. We can let you in, now that the birthday girl has unwrapped her present a bit earlier than we expected.'

'You weren't supposed to see him till the barbecue, when all your friends were here,' chided her mum.

'What? Were you going to jump out of my birthday cake? Ta-raa!' Jill struck an extravagant pose.

'Thankfully, no,' he said. 'I was just going to arrive when you were opening your presents.'

'Not even gift-wrapped?' Jill joked.

'Whatever made you go down to the sleep-out?' asked Patricia. 'We thought he was quite safe hiding there till tonight.'

'I heard him whistling,' she confessed, 'and I knew right away who it was.' She smiled happily and hugged him. 'The best birthday present ever.'

'And it's all thanks to Linda,' explained Andrew. 'She brought me to my senses, and arranged the whole thing.'

'We picked him up from the airport yesterday while you and Judy were shopping,' giggled Patricia. 'And smuggled him back here. Judy couldn't bring you back till we texted her the all-clear.'

'So, she was in this, too!' said Jill.

'Of course. Now, I'm sure you'll be hungry,' said Patricia. ''Come and eat some breakfast.'

The older women couldn't help but notice the change in Jill. She was laughing and bubbling over with excitement, her eyes shone, and her whole body seemed to have come alive in the space of a few hours.

'You were right,' Patricia murmured to Linda, as they cleared away the breakfast dishes. 'Best birthday present ever.'

'Nice bit of match-making, even if I do say so myself. He just needed some plain speaking and some sense knocked into him.' Linda vigorously scrubbed at the pan where she'd cooked scrambled eggs for the young couple.

'How on earth did you manage it?' asked Patricia.

'Oh,' said Linda with a wry smile, as she remembered the scathing email she'd sent Andrew, 'just dropped a wee word in his ear. Let him know how much Jill was missing him.'

32

The birthday party was in full swing. The heat of the day had gone, and the smell of barbecuing lamb chops and sausages, tiger prawns and Moreton Bay bugs, drifted across the paddock. Tables were laden with salads and rice dishes, olives and pastas, while bottles of beer sat in the cool boxes filled with ice. Some of Jill's friends had brought guitars and drums to set up an impromptu band, while people sat around with plates laden with food, or sang along and danced to the music.

An enormous pile of presents was building up under one of the gum trees, and Jill was adding another to the heap when Andrew took her hand and led her aside to a quiet spot.

'I haven't given you my present yet,' he said, putting his hand into the pocket of his shorts and bringing out a small, but beautifully wrapped, gift.

'I thought you were my present,' Jill said, pulling the silver ribbon to open it. 'I wasn't expecting anything else. After all, what could top finding you here?'

She pulled a small velvet box from its wrapping, and

opened it. Inside, nestling on its bed of red silk, was a diamond solitaire ring. Jill gasped as the stone's facets flashed and sparkled in the light.

'Will you marry me, Jill?' said Andrew, looking into her eyes.

She met his gaze. 'Yes,' she breathed. 'Oh yes!'

Carefully, Andrew lifted out the ring and slipped it onto Jill's finger.

'Let's make it soon,' he said. 'Where will we have it? Here or in Scotland?'

'Did you bring your kilt?'

'Actually, yes, I did,' he admitted. 'Although, in this heat, I wouldn't last long in it.'

'Well then, what are we waiting for?'

'Don't you need a dress? And flowers? And things?'

'I've got you,' she answered. 'What more do I need?'

AND SO, a few weeks later, under the shade of the gum trees in the paddock, Jill Marcia Kennedy plighted her troth to Andrew James MacCallum-Blair. The bride wore a simple white dress and carried a bouquet of Australian flowers – wattle and bottlebrush and Sturt peas – while the bridegroom wore his kilt, with a plain white shirt in deference to the heat.

Their friends and family partied under the trees until it was time for the young couple to head to the airport.

Tears and kisses were exchanged, and promises of visits to Scotland were made by almost all the people there. Linda and Patricia were to be first; Linda explained that when she returned to Edinburgh in January, she would bring Jill's mum with her.

'…and we'll have the best party our close has ever seen.

Invite everybody, and wear my green chiffon again. I want to see how super you looked in it.'

At last, they were on their way. 'We'll have our first Christmas and Hogmanay in Scotland,' Andrew said, as he drove their hired car to the airport. 'It's quite something, Hogmanay in Edinburgh. It's the biggest street party in the world. And the fireworks display is awesome.'

'Fireworks again,' murmured Jill, as she twirled her new wedding ring on her finger. 'Life with you is always fireworks.'

'Long may it continue to be so, Mrs. MacCallum-Blair,' replied Andrew.

They smiled happily and headed to the airport and the flight to Scotland, a set of crutches safely tucked away in the trunk and with the name of the hospital in Edinburgh written on the label.

About the Author

I've been a writer ever since I was a child and I've written all kinds of things. I started off writing for children, producing a Postman Pat story for a comic every week for five years; I've written over 100 radio and TV scripts for BBC children's programmes and along the way, I've had short stories and articles published in many magazines as well as online.

I came to novel writing late; I did a Masters in Creative Writing and decided that for my dissertation it was easier to write a novel rather than ten different short stories. So I wrote *Loving Mother* about a mother and her daughter and the arrival of someone claiming to be the mother's child that she gave up at birth. It's still available on Amazon.

I now live on the east coast of Scotland after many years on the west.

INTERVIEW WITH THE AUTHOR

Festival Fireworks **is set mainly in Edinburgh. Why did you choose that city for your novel?**

I've visited Edinburgh many times through the years and worked there one summer during the festival. Now I'm lucky enough to actually live within 40 minutes of the city. It's such a fascinating place; there's always something going on and so much history going back centuries. You can almost feel it seeping out of its buildings.

And of course, it's the must-visit place for tourists to Scotland so it was obvious that Jill would visit, as well as having a family connection there.

Andrew seems a sensitive soul who is dealing with some issues in his life. He's not a stereotypical alpha male, is he?

I think that type of male is outdated now and belongs in the past. Before, it was all muscles and stiff upper lip and that doesn't chime with today's idea of the ideal man. He's not perfect by any means but that's what I think makes him interesting.

Aunt Linda plays a sterling role behind the scenes in bringing them together – eventually. Would it have happened without her intervention/interference?

She certainly gives them a nudge in the right direction, or in some situations, a hefty shove. I enjoyed writing Linda, she's someone I might perhaps revisit in another book and tell her story.

Jill returns to Australia. How did you research that setting?

I didn't have to as I lived there for several years and have been back many times since. Aussies are great travellers – we've had many visitors to Scotland over the years; when I opened our front door one morning, there was one of our friends patiently waiting for us to get up as he'd arrived unexpectedly on the milk train!

Do you enjoy engaging with your readers?

Yes, I love meeting them and hearing their views on what I've written, especially if they've left a review on Amazon or Bookbub or any other book site. And they can follow me on Facebook at Ann Burnett Author, or on my website and blog, annburnett.co.uk.

What other novels have you written?

At the moment I'm in the process of bringing out new editions of them all but readers might enjoy my collection of prize-winning short stories, *Take a Leaf Out of My Book.* There's something for everyone in it; as it says on the blurb, *Meet the inept Glasgow private eye, find out about Ped Xing and share a young girl's suffering in a war-torn country.*

ACKNOWLEDGMENTS

Many thanks are due to Sheila Grant, Sheila Johnston and Rosemary Gemmell whose comments, advice and encouragement were much appreciated. And to Claire Wingfield for sitting next to me at lunch and starting this process off.

Lightning Source UK Ltd.
Milton Keynes UK
UKHW022115210220
359134UK00009B/671